"Do I detect a faint note of criticism?"

Philip shrugged at her question. "Not really. I realize you don't have much sense of family responsibility, so I suppose you've done well to stand it this long."

Nell breathed hard but managed to control herself. "Not many young people do nowadays," he added thoughtfully and stuck a cigarette between his lips. "Mind if I smoke?" He lighted up and gave her a sardonic smile. "Haven't you any vices, doctor?"

"Of course I have, Mr. Trent. I'm selfish and self-centered. I don't care about my family—" She broke off, furious with herself for letting her tongue run away. "Isn't that what you think of me?" she added crossly, and was even more annoyed when he laughed.

"You said it, my dear! Conscience pricking, perhaps?"

Return to Lanmore

by

SHEILA DOUGLAS

Harlequin Books

TORONTO • LONDON • NEW YORK • AMSTERDAM
SYDNEY • HAMBURG • PARIS • STOCKHOLM

Original hardcover edition published in 1979
by Mills & Boon Limited

ISBN 0-373-02336-7

Harlequin edition published June 1980

CHAPTER ONE

'I THINK you should come today, Nell. At once, if you want to see your grandfather alive.'

Nell's hand tightened on the telephone receiver and she stared blindly at the corridor wall. She had known Dr MacFarlane all her life and he was not the man to exaggerate, or to panic. If he said her grandfather's heart attack was a serious one then it was.

'Is he in hospital?' she asked.

'Yes. The intensive care unit at Barnslow General. Your aunt called me at five o'clock this morning.'

'Conscious?'

'A little confused, though that's mainly due to sedation.'

'But he asked to see me?' No answer. 'Dr MacFarlane, he does want to see me?'

'I'm sure he does, my dear.' After forty years in England the doctor's voice still had a pronounced Scots accent. Now it deepened and became persuasive. 'Maybe I'm an old fool, stepping in where no one else dares, but don't you think it's time you made things up with your grandfather? If it's not too late already,' he added sombrely.

Nell pushed a hand through her curly brown hair and tugged at it distractedly. 'But if I come down and he doesn't want to see me, mightn't that make him worse?'

'Naturally we shall ask him first.'

'What does Aunt Elizabeth say?'

Again a pause. 'I have not consulted Elizabeth,' said Dr MacFarlane. 'You must make up your own mind. But if you don't come you'll be sorry afterwards. When it's too late.'

'Oh, don't say that!' cried Nell, near to tears. 'Of course

I'm coming—I was just afraid of upsetting him. I'll come at once. I should be down about midday, and I'll go straight to the hospital.'

'Telephone me when you arrive, and I'll try to join you. If I can't I'll leave a message with switchboard. Goodbye, my dear.'

Nell put the receiver down and walked back slowly into the dining-room. She had been in the middle of a late breakfast when one of the maids had summoned her to the telephone. Because it was nine o'clock on a weekday morning the doctors' dining-room was empty of all but a scattering of people. Most of the resident medical staff at Queen's College Hospital were already on the wards, or in Outpatients or the operating theatre. Only the lucky few who were off duty, or like Nell and her friends, who were going on holiday, could allow themselves the luxury of a late breakfast.

She sat down again at the table and Belinda Stokes, who was her best friend, looked at her concernedly. 'What's wrong, Nell? Bad news?'

The two men were staring at her too—Jimmy Green, who was Belinda's boy-friend, and Ted Wilding, who was the fourth member of their little group. She knew them all well, had spent five years at medical school with them, and had just completed her pre-registration year at Q.C.H. in their company. She told them what had happened, and because they knew that she had quarrelled with her grandfather and cut herself off from home, she didn't have to go into great detail.

'Of course you'll have to visit him,' Belinda agreed. 'Whatever sort of reception he gives you.'

'How long since you saw your family?' asked Ted, and Nell sighed.

'Too long.' She eyed her plate of congealed bacon and eggs with distaste, pushed it away and drank tepid coffee. 'Over five years. Ever since we started at medical school.'

That had been the original cause of the quarrel, her decision to become a doctor. When she had been a little girl, pretty and amenable, she had been the apple of her grandfather's eye. Nell had been brought up by Colonel Whitehead after her parents had been killed in a plane crash. She scarcely remembered them, and the time when she hadn't lived in her grandfather's house. Aunt Elizabeth, his younger and unmarried daughter, had been the third member of the family, but her relationship with Nell had never been a warm one.

'Well, I'm sorry the old boy's ill,' observed Jimmy, 'but it's not your fault there's been this rift.'

'And you did try to make it up,' observed Belinda. 'Do eat something. You can't drive on an empty stomach.'

Nell shook her head. 'I can't face food,' but she poured herself another cup of coffee. She kept her head down and stirred vigorously, because she didn't want them to see the tears in her eyes. The memory of those telephone calls which had got nowhere, of those letters which hadn't been answered, still had the power to hurt her badly.

'Your grandfather must be positively prehistoric,' Ted remarked. 'A girl chooses her own career these days. After all, you got a grant. You didn't cost him a penny.'

'It was nothing to do with expense,' Nell murmured, and gave her nose a quick blow. 'Grandpa's old-fashioned. He doesn't approve of career women, and especially women in medicine.'

'So O.K., he doesn't approve. That's no reason for the old idiot to quarrel with you. In my opinion he behaved like something out of a Victorian novel.'

'He is like something out of a Victorian novel,' Nell agreed, with a faint smile. Impossible to explain to her friends, who came from such different backgrounds, her grandfather's attitude to women.

'Fool thing wasting your time in the sixth form,' he had growled when she announced her intention of doing

A-levels. 'Never thought you'd pass 'em,' had been his comment when she achieved very creditable grades in Chemistry, Physics and Biology. It was only then that Nell had told him and Aunt Elizabeth that she had applied and been accepted at a London medical school. She hadn't done so until she knew she was successful, because she had wanted to present them with a fait accompli.

'No granddaughter of mine is going to become a doctor,' the Colonel had stormed, for all the world as if Nell had wanted to take up some highly dubious career. 'The women in our family have never needed to work. The idea's ridiculous.'

'It's not ridiculous, Grandpa.' At first Nell had thought this extraordinary attitude a joke, and had been patient with the irascible old man, but quietly determined not to give way. 'Everyone works nowadays, and I've always wanted to be a doctor.'

'You kept very quiet about it, miss. Not been exactly honest with us, have you?'

'I didn't say anything because I knew how it would be. I'm sorry you don't like the idea, but you'll have to get used to it.'

'Never! You will write and tell these people'—the old man had thumped Nell's letter of acceptance with scorn—'that you've changed your mind. You don't want their vacancy.'

When Nell said she wouldn't he had gone an alarming shade of red, shouted that she was just like her father and that he wished to heaven that his daughter had never married that impossible man. Upset by these remarks about her parents, Nell had lost her temper too. It had ended with the Colonel storming that if she went off to London she needn't come back, and that was exactly what had happened. She had not visited her home in Shropshire, nor seen either her grandfather or her aunt for over five years. Several members of the family and one or two old friends, including Dr MacFarlane, had tried to patch up the quarrel, without success.

'Would you like me to run you down?' suggested Ted. 'I've done my packing.'

The four of them had arranged a skiing holiday in Switzerland as a celebration of the fact that they were now fully registered doctors. They were flying from London Airport that night, at least the others would be. Nell would not be going with them.

'It's sweet of you, Ted, but I'll manage. Though you could ring the airport and ask about a refund.'

They all stared at her. 'You could be back in plenty of time,' said Ted. 'It's no distance to Barnslow on the motorway.'

When she explained that there was no question of going on holiday he looked very upset. It was only recently that he and Nell had started going out together, although they had been good friends for years. Nell liked him enormously, admired his qualities as a doctor, and had been looking forward to their holiday foursome. What she wasn't quite sure about yet was just how much Ted really meant to her. Could an easy student friendship ripen into love after so many years? And just how serious was Ted about her?

Very serious, it seemed, to judge by the violence of his reaction. His pleasant face was flushed, his jaw set at an aggressive angle, as he tried to make her change her mind. 'You owe the old man nothing, Nell. He's behaved abominably to you. So O.K., go and see him, even stay a day or two. But fly out and join us later. Please!'

He laid a hand on her arm, his blue eyes beseeching. Belinda and Jimmy exchanged a look and disappeared tactfully.

'I might come out later,' Nell agreed. 'It—it depends what happens.' If her grandfather died there would be no point in staying on, but if he recovered against all expectations, and wanted her around, then she would spend her holiday in her old home. When she told Ted this he looked sulky and very young.

'It's a rotten thing to happen, just now when I thought——' He stuck on that, then started again. 'I've had a thing about you for years, Nell, but you never showed any interest. Then when Belle suggested this foursome it seemed like a chance at last. A chance for us to really get to know each other.'

A little dismayed by his intensity, because she was far from sure of her own feelings, Nell smiled at him and tried for a light reply. 'We do know each other, Ted. We ought to after all we've been through together. Remember that first day at Queen's College? I felt terribly shy and nervous. You were the first person who spoke to me. I've never forgotten it.'

His answering smile was warm, his ill humour completely banished. 'Nor have I. You were such a sweet kid, with those big brown eyes and that innocent look about you. I wasn't the only one who wanted to take care of you.'

Nell had had more than her share of boy-friends in her years at medical school, none of them very serious, none of them capable of distracting her from her studies. She rose from the table. 'I really must be off. I'll ring you early evening and let you know what's happening. And I am sorry to have disrupted our plans. You'll have to find a nice Swiss girl, or you'll be the odd man out!'

She left then, ran up to her room in the residents' quarters and snatched up the suitcase which was already labelled for her holiday. As she made her way to the car park, she thought wryly that the thick sweaters and trousers she had packed for the ski slopes, would be most welcome in her grandfather's house. January at Lanmore Manor could be bitterly cold, for Colonel Whitehead belonged to that generation of Englishmen who despised central heating, though perhaps advancing years had mellowed his outlook. In five years there were bound to be changes.

Nell slung her case on to the back seat of her Mini and slid into the driving seat.

Ted's remark about it being no distance to Barnslow might be correct, but she lost her way in the suburbs of North London and took a frustrating hour to reach the motorway, so that it was past one o'clock before she turned on to the Barnslow exit. Then she took a wrong turning on the outskirts of the town, and finally arrived at the hospital at one-thirty, tired, hungry and apprehensive.

As she walked through the swing doors, Dr MacFarlane came out of a room on the far side of the entrance hall. 'Nell, my dear!' He took her hands in a strong grip, looked searchingly down at her. 'How you've changed! You're a young woman now.'

Was he talking like this because he didn't want to give her bad news? 'Grandpa?' faltered Nell, and her legs began to shake.

'Holding his own. Making a fight of it, though he's by no means out of danger. He's sleeping now, but they'll call you as soon as he wakes up.'

Relief made her sag against him and he put an arm around her shoulders to comfort her. 'Had any lunch? I thought not. There should be something left.'

He took her to the doctors' dining-room, introduced her to some of his colleagues as Colonel Whitehead's grand-daughter, and plied her with ham sandwiches and fresh coffee. Everyone else had left before she finished. As Nell drank her second cup she became aware that Dr MacFarlane's manner was a little constrained. He was either tired, having been got out of bed very early this morning, or not as friendly as she remembered him being in the past.

'How did you know where to find me?' she asked.

'I knew where you trained, my dear, so I rang the Dean's office and asked them for help. I'm pleased to know that they regarded your work highly enough to give you a job at Queen's.'

Only there was no warmth in his voice, which would have made the small compliment more worthwhile. 'What did Grandpa say when he knew I was coming?'

'About time! With which I entirely agree.' Dr Mac-Farlane's voice was dry, his expression severe.

Nell flushed. 'I'd have come before if I'd thought I was wanted.'

'Really, Nell!' He pushed his spectacles down to peer at her, bushy grey eyebrows drawn together in a frown. 'That's a silly thing to say, and you know it.'

Not liking to be thought insincere, Nell persisted in this theme. 'I did try to make it up. Honestly.'

He pulled out his pipe and tobacco pouch. 'Shall we leave it? No point raking up old quarrels, especially at a time like this.'

So he didn't believe her, and the thought made her feel even more wretched. 'Is Aunt Elizabeth here?' she asked.

'She went home for lunch. She should be back soon.'

'Did she want me to come?'

'I should say she was neutral.' Again that dry note in his voice.

Nell swallowed the last of her coffee and stood up. 'Could we go along to the intensive care unit? I'll sit outside if he's not ready to see me.'

There was a small room for the relatives of patients in the I.C.U., empty when Nell went in, for which she felt profoundly relieved. It gave her a few minutes to get a grip on herself before the painful meeting with her grandfather, and the possible embarrassment of seeing Aunt Elizabeth. Dr MacFarlane's tone had implied that her aunt was not disposed to be friendly. Did everyone blame her for the quarrel? Had she in truth been more at fault than she cared to admit? If she had been more tactful, not lost her temper so furiously, perhaps the old man could have been talked round into accepting her career.

She was so deep in thought, hand to forehead, eyes on the ground, that she didn't hear the waiting-room door open. 'Hallo, Nell!' Her aunt's voice roused her and she looked up quickly.

Elizabeth Whitehead looked young for her age, light brown hair coiled on the nape of her neck, skin smooth and cared for, figure trim. Behind her stood a man whom Nell had never seen before, a big man, for he topped Elizabeth by a head and she wasn't a short woman. An impressive-looking man whom you wouldn't forget if you had ever met him. Nell stared at them both, dismayed by her aunt's cool manner, which was just this side of being downright unfriendly.

They came into the room and Elizabeth introduced the stranger. 'Philip Trent, a neighbour of ours. And this is my niece, Nell.' My difficult niece, her tone implied, or was Nell being over-sensitive?

She shook hands with Philip Trent, wondering why he had come, and he looked down at her unsmilingly, so that the beginning of a smile on Nell's face wavered and disappeared.

'I was so upset this morning that I could never have coped on my own.' Elizabeth fluttered well kept hands and gave a warm glance up at Mr Trent. 'I'm so *bad* with illness. Medical people must be very hard.'

Recognising this as a dig in her direction, Nell said quietly that one tried to be detached, which wasn't the same as being hard. Her aunt ignored this. 'Now about Father. I shall go in first. Make sure he really wants to see you.'

She moved towards the door. Philip Trent sat down, stretching long legs before him, and stared fixedly at a picture on the opposite wall. The tactlessness of the man! He might have guessed that she would have welcomed a few words alone with her aunt. If he had brought

Elizabeth to the hospital, he was probably intimate enough to be aware of the family set-up.

'How long have you known my aunt, Mr Trent?' Some of Nell's irritation must have shown in her voice, for he gave her a straight look.

'For nearly as long as you've stayed away, Miss Ramsay.' The words were quietly spoken, but none the less a rebuke. Nell was prepared to put up with censure from Dr MacFarlane, however little deserved, but not from a stranger.

'And I call *that* an unnecessary remark!' she exclaimed hotly. 'But tact doesn't seem to be your strong point.'

His eyes narrowed. He leant forward in his chair, and Nell shifted away from him. What a hard face he had! What an uncomfortably direct glance! 'You're wondering why I'm here, Miss Ramsay? Not from choice, I assure you. I drove Elizabeth back to the hospital just now, and she didn't feel up to meeting you on her own.' He sat back again and resumed his study of the very ordinary landscape behind Nell's head. She was already regretting that ill-considered remark, which she would never have made if she hadn't been so tense and unhappy. When she stammered a sort of apology he flicked her an indifferent glance, but before he could say anything Elizabeth returned.

'Father's awake and expecting you, Nell.' She accompanied her niece to the door of the intensive care unit, urging Nell to be tactful, to say as little as possible, not to upset the old man. Had she always been as irritating?

'All right, Aunt Elizabeth, I won't say a thing out of line. As if I would at a time like this!'

She had been many times into an I.C.U. She should have been prepared for what she found, but the frail figure in the bed with bloodless face and sunken eyes bore no resemblance to the grandfather she remembered. He lay quite flat, one pillow under his head, palms down on the white counterpane, one arm fixed to an intravenous drip, an oxygen cylinder near the head of the bed. The staff nurse sitting beside him rose and moved towards the window. Colonel Whitehead's faded eyes watched Nell with a total lack of expression.

'Oh, Grandpa!' She sank down beside him on to the chair the nurse had vacated, laid her young hand over his pitifully thin one, and couldn't say another thing.

'Nell ...' It was the merest thread of sound, and the shrunken hand beneath hers moved a fraction.

She gripped it more tightly, fighting against tears. 'For God's sake don't cry,' the Colonel managed in a fierce whisper. A flicker of a smile crossed his worn face. 'Had enough of that from Elizabeth!'

'Oh, Grandpa!' She raised his hand gently and held it against her cheek, and the nurse rustled watchfully in the background. 'Don't talk. I'll just sit with you for as long as they'll let me.'

All the bitterness of the last five years had blown away before the overwhelming fact that this was the person she had once loved best in the world, and looking at him now she was convinced he hadn't long to live. Five minutes was all the Sister in charge allowed her. Back in the waiting-room, Nell blew her nose and asked Elizabeth what she planned to do now.

'Stay until teatime, but you'd better go back to the house. You look fagged out.' For the first time her manner became a little less chilly. 'And you too, Philip. I've caused you quite enough inconvenience.'

'Nonsense, Elizabeth. I'll stay if you want me to.'

When she insisted that he leave, he offered to return for her later. 'Please don't bother. I'll get a taxi, or if Nell went with you I could borrow her car.'

It seemed the obvious solution, so Nell didn't like to demur. Ten minutes later Philip Trent and she were heading south away from Barnslow and into the Shropshire hills. He made no attempt to break the silence between them. When Nell felt she couldn't bear it any longer she tried a friendly gesture.

'Aunt Elizabeth was right—we are putting you to a lot of trouble.'

'Of course you're not. I look on your grandfather and Elizabeth as very good friends.'

'Where do you live, Mr Trent?' she asked.

'You can see my chimneys from the top floor of your grandfather's house.' He turned his head for a moment and gave her a faint smile. At her puzzled expression he added quietly, 'There've been a good many changes since you were here last.'

Disquieted by his words, Nell asked him what he meant. 'Has Grandpa been cutting down trees?' But even then the only houses in view would be farmworkers' cottages. Mr Trent, with his elegant clothes and unmistakable air of affluence, couldn't live in one of those.

'I bought some land from your grandfather,' he said casually. 'I liked this area, but I couldn't find just what I wanted, so I built my own house.'

The idea of a modern building within sight of the centuries-old manor house upset Nell deeply. What could have happened to her grandfather, to make him part with even an acre of his beloved land?

'Don't worry. You can only just see my place from the attics.' He was openly amused by her reaction.

She stared out of the window at the familiar shape of the Long Mynd, looming dark and forbidding on this grey January day. Changes there might be, but the hills were eternal, the countryside was beautiful. When they turned off the A-road into the familiar lanes of her childhood, walked and ridden over so many times, Nell felt a lump in her throat, it was so good to be back. Then they were into Lanmore village with its Norman church and its single store, out again in seconds, and a minute or two later driving past the sign that said 'Lanmore Manor only. No through road.'

The home farm lay at the head of the lane, looking in better condition than when Nell had last seen it. She craned her neck to study two new buildings that hadn't been there before. 'Do you know when Grandpa put those up? When I left he was cutting back on the farm.'

There had been endless trouble trying to find a good manager once the old one had retired, and Aunt Elizabeth had been in favour of reducing the livestock.

'I put them up, not your grandfather,' and at her astonished stare, 'I told you there'd been changes. Haven't you kept in touch at all?'

She had kept in touch for a time with childhood friends, but in the way of it they had drifted apart, first the letters reduced to Christmas cards, latterly nothing. 'Do you mean you—you've gone into partnership with Grandpa?' She waited anxiously for his reply, which was a moment or two in coming.

'My dear girl, can you see the old man in parnership with anybody?' He smiled rather grimly at the idea. 'No, I bought the farm from him. I think he was glad to get rid of it.'

Lanmore Manor had belonged to Whiteheads since Elizabethan times. The Colonel had a fierce pride of possession, an intense love of the land. Nell swallowed and said in a small voice, 'How could he be glad to get rid of it? He loved it so.'

In a more kindly tone than he had used to her until now, he tried to explain. 'So many of these old estates have fallen on hard times. Death duties over the generations, the rising cost of maintenance, soaring wages. If he'd had a son I suppose he'd have hung on somehow, but he didn't think it was worth it. Neither you or your aunt could possibly have run the place at a profit.'

They had reached the end of the park now and were

running between rhododendron bushes, which had grown out of hand since Nell had last seen them. Then they rounded a bend and there was the house, built in the early years of Elizabeth's reign. At least that looked the same, thought Nell thankfully, as Philip Trent drew up on the forecourt near the great front door. She took him up on his last remark before she got out of the car.

'If Grandpa couldn't make a profit on the farm how can you?'

He switched off the ignition, removed his driving gloves and turned to face her. 'I don't,' he said, 'though I hope to some day. At the moment the farm's more a hobby than a business venture.'

A man who could afford to run two thousand acres without profit and yet keep it in such excellent repair, must be very rich indeed. Nell wondered what his real work was, if in fact he did work, but didn't like to ask. A property developer perhaps? The thought was appalling. Good manners made her invite him in, but she was relieved when he shook his head.

'Thank you, but I've a lot to do.'

At such close quarters she was very conscious of his looks. Thick dark hair and alert grey eyes. Eyes which seemed to sum her up and find her wanting, to make her ill at ease and awkward.

'Goodbye then,' she said stiffly. As she was getting out of the car the front door opened and Miss Black, who had been the housekeeper for as long as Nell could remember, stood there expectantly, a query on her face.

'Blackie! Grandpa's no worse, but he's still critically ill. Oh, Blackie, it's good to see you!'

The housekeeper's anxious expression changed to one of pleasure. 'You too, Nell dear. I'm so glad you've come home.'

What a contrast to Elizabeth's welcome! Nell gave the old woman a hug, and they clung together for a moment.

Then she became aware of Mr Trent, who had taken her suitcase from the boot, standing beside them and watching this touching scene impassively.

'Thank you,' she said hastily, disengaging herself from Blackie's embrace.

'I'll carry it in for you.'

'No need—I can manage.' She snatched up her suitcase and with a shrug he turned away.

'Wouldn't he like a cup of tea?' Blackie asked.

'He said he wanted to get off.' They watched the blue Aston Martin disappear round a bend in the drive, then went into the house. Nell stared around her at the oak-panelled hall with the stuffed deer's heads she had always hated, and the portraits of Whitehead ancestors about whom she had made up so many stories as a child.

'Thank goodness this is the same,' she muttered. 'Who *is* Mr Trent, Blackie, and why did Grandpa sell him the farm?'

'Because he needed the money,' Blackie said with devastating directness. 'You don't think he would have parted with it for any other reason, do you?'

'But couldn't he have found someone—well, nicer—to be such a near neighbour?'

'Mr Trent made him a very generous offer,' said Blackie with a touch of dryness. 'The Colonel wasn't in a position to refuse. Besides, it's turned out very well. We all like him, even your grandfather, once he got used to a stranger on his land.'

'Then he must have mellowed in the last few years!'

'Not really. Just got too old and tired to care.' Blackie herself bore the marks of increasing years. She wore spectacles now and her white hair was less abundant, and —'You're thinner, I think,' said Nell.

'Yes, I suppose I am, but more healthy at my age, don't you think? And are you really a doctor? It's hard to credit it.'

Later they had tea in the housekeeper's room, where Nell had always been welcome as a child, and which was far cosier than the family's rooms. She curled up in the big armchair by the fire, while Blackie chose her favourite straight-backed one, saying that it was easier to get out of, for she was stiffer than ever these days. She brought Nell up to date on local affairs and the changes on the estate. Mr Trent was not a property developer. He was a business man, whose headquarters were in London, though he was planning to move them to the West Midlands as soon as possible.

'What sort of business?' asked Nell.

'Engineering, I think,' Blackie said vaguely. 'Your aunt will know if you're interested. They're very friendly.'

'So I've noticed. I hope he's not often around?'

Blackie's lips pursed. 'Quite often, and what's wrong with that? He drops in to play chess with your grandfather. He entertains a good deal too. In fact you might say that he's quite a leading member of local society.'

'I don't doubt it, with all that money,' said Nell with unusual cynicism. The man had an irritating air of assurance about him, a cool authority that would probably have put her back up, even if they hadn't exchanged those sharp remarks when they first met.

'Oh no, dear,' Blackie said firmly. 'It's not just his money, though they do say he has plenty of it. Mr Trent's a gentleman, anyone can see that.'

'Yes, I suppose he is. For goodness' sake, can't we talk about something more intereting?'

'No need to snap at me,' Blackie reproved, just as she might have spoken to the young Nell many years ago. 'It was you who wanted to know about Mr Trent, after all.'

Elizabeth Whitehead came home shortly after five, with the news that her father was showing signs of recovery. 'I talked to the heart specialist and for the first time they're hopeful. But it *is* no more than that—only a chance.'

Nell was thankful that her aunt showed no inclination to be sociable. They were not at ease with each other. They had never been close, and the five years they had been apart were difficult to bridge. So it was a relief when Elizabeth announced that she was going to have a bath and get into bed, for she had been on the go since five o'clock that morning.

'If I could have something light on a tray, Blackie, Nell can bring it up.'

In the old days there had been a living-in maid. Now Blackie managed with a girl from the village. When she had taken her aunt's supper up to the bedroom, Nell climbed the narrow stairs to what had once been the servants' bedrooms. Even in her childhood most of the rooms had been empty, and she had played in them with her friends, when the weather had been too bad to go outside. She went into the end room, which had always been her favourite, crossed to the window and looked out across the park. In the distance, perhaps half a mile away, lights twinkled from behind a belt of trees.

Philip Trent's house! In the morning she would have a closer look at it. Now it was time to join Blackie for supper. She went slowly downstairs, her thoughts with her grandfather, praying that his recovery would be maintained, and that he would still be alive in the morning.

CHAPTER TWO

NELL woke at seven, and finding it difficult to settle decided to telephone the hospital. She padded downstairs through the cold dark house and used the line in her grandfather's study, so that she wouldn't wake the other two women. When the switchboard man learnt that she was a doctor, he put her on to the night superintendent.

The news was good. Colonel Whitehead's general condition was much improved, his blood pressure rising again, his pulse rate slowing. Nell listened carefully to the medical details, thanked the superintendent and went into the kitchen to make herself some coffee. It was the original old kitchen, though it had been modernised some forty years ago—shabby but comfortable, with a solid fuel stove. The two Labradors, who slept by the stove, left their baskets to greet her, both young dogs, descended from Honey, whom Nell had adored in her childhood.

When she had drunk her coffee and eaten two slices of toast, the first pale light of the winter morning was brightening the sky. She felt too restless to go back to bed, so she pulled on thick clothes and a pair of rubber boots, and set out across the park in the direction of Philip Trent's house. The Labradors went with her, friends already after only a few hours' acquaintance, tails waving their pleasure at this unexpected outing.

The air had a bite to it although there was no wind. Nell dug her hands deep into the pockets of her old duffle coat, for she had forgotten her gloves. She reached the copse behind which she thought Mr Trent's house must lie, and climbed the stile into the little wood, to follow a narrow twisting path which ended at a second stile. There

she stopped and stared for a long time at what had once
been open fields, sloping down to the river on her right.

She had to admit that the house looked surprisingly
mellow, not brick as she had feared, but built of the local
stone—a long low building, looking not unlike a prosperous
farmhouse, which she supposed it was, even if Mr Trent
was only a part time farmer. The bulk of the gardens lay
behind the house, between it and the wood, and again they
looked remarkably mature, with evergreen trees and shrubs
attractively disposed, and more formal beds close to the
house. Ranger's ears pricked suddenly and he gave a low
growl. Seconds later Nell heard a horse's hooves, coming
from the direction of the river.

The house was still in darkness, but someone was up,
perhaps a farm worker. Not wanting to be seen, she
walked quickly back through the copse, calling to the dogs.
Ranger loped after her, but Paddy, who had found a gap
into the field at the bottom of the garden, seemed to be
having trouble in returning. He barked to draw her
attention to his plight, then relapsed into an insistent whine.
The horse's hooves sounded nearer. Nell ran back and
found Paddy stuck halfway through the hedge.

'You're too fat,' she told him crossly. 'Come on, boy!
Come on!'

Tugging at his collar brought it off in Nell's hand, and
Paddy managed to extricate himself backwards, just as
the horseman came round the corner of the wood. It
was Philip Trent, riding a fine chestnut mare. It would
be, thought Nell, discomfited at being caught spying out
the land.

His eyebrows went up when he saw her. 'Hallo! You're
an early bird!'

'So are you!' she retorted crossly. 'This was always
one of my favourite walks.'

At this gratuitous piece of information, which was not
even true, he smiled and dismounted. 'Really?' The

smile was disbelieving. 'Sure you weren't just indulging your curiosity? Understandable under the circumstances,' he added quite kindly. 'And how's the old man? Did you ring the hospital before you came out?'

'Better,' Nell said briefly. Patronising beast! She glared at him, taking in the polo-necked Fair Isle sweater and the immaculate fawn breeches, which must have cost a small fortune. Her temper wasn't improved by the fact that beside his casual elegance she felt positively dowdy in the old duffle coat, which was a left-over from her schooldays, and the green knitted cap which she had found on a peg in the cloakroom. It was a size too large for her and kept slipping down on her forehead. She pushed it back, and a strand of brown hair came loose, falling into her eyes. While she was fiddling with it Philip Trent lifted up Paddy with surprising ease and manoeuvred him over the stile. Then he turned his attention to Nell.

'Allow me.' He brushed the hair out of her eyes and tucked it under the old green cap, for all the world as if she was child. Then he stood back to study her, that maddening smile hovering round his lips. 'I find it hard to believe you're a qualified doctor. You look about sixteen in that get-up!'

Nell kicked at a pile of fallen leaves with her rubber boot, for all the world as if she *was* still a child. Something about this man made her feel a gauche immature schoolgirl again, an unaccustomed feeling that did nothing to endear him to her. 'Do I?'

Her cool tone had no effect. 'I expect you look different when you're on duty. Women doctors can be alarmingly efficient.'

His choice of words suggested to Nell that he was of the same breed as her grandfather, old-fashioned in his outlook on her sex, with less excuse since he couldn't be more than forty. Considerably less, she amended. A few years younger than her aunt probably, who was only just thirty-nine. Yesterday she had thought him older, but now in the clear morning light, he looked about the same age as some of the registrars at her hospital.

'Well?' he asked casually, gesturing towards his house. 'What do you think of it?'

She would have liked to deflate him with a critical remark, but being an honest girl, she spoke the truth, after only a moment's hesitation. It's better than I expected. New houses can be such terrible eyesores. And your garden's lovely. Not too formal, not just a jungle. Like ours,' she added ruefully.

He looked pleased and surprised. 'Praise indeed,' he said wryly. 'I quite expected you to damn it entirely. I'm not too fond of old houses myself, having been brought up in one. Woodworm and dry rot and leaking roofs! You can have them!'

The practical sort of attitude a man like him would have. Nell stooped to fasten Paddy's collar again. 'Keep still, you stupid dog! Your horse will wander, Mr Trent.'

'No, she won't. She's well trained. And couldn't you drop the formality, Nell?' Her name came easily from his lips. 'We're neighbours after all; and bound to see a good deal of each other. That is if you're staying?'

'I shall stay as long as Grandpa wants me to.'

'And that might be longer than any of us expected,' he said quietly. 'I'm so glad there's an improvement.' There was no doubt that he was sincerely concerned about the Colonel, and he had certainly been both kind and helpful to Elizabeth. Nell looked at him with more tolerant eyes, wondering if she had judged him too hastily.

'I'd better get back,' she said, calling the dogs from where they were rooting through the bushes. 'Goodbye, Mr—goodbye, Philip.' She said his name a little shyly, and was annoyed with herself because of it.

'Tell Elizabeth I'll look in this evening,' he called after
her, and Nell nodded, trudging off through the wood,
crunching over the ice-covered leaves on the narrow path.

When she passed on Philip's message at breakfast, her
aunt looked pleased. 'He's been an absolute brick. I don't
know how I'd have managed without him.'

'Is he on holiday?'

Elizabeth shook her head. 'I don't think so. Why?'

'Then is he so rich he doesn't need to work?' asked
Nell with a touch of sarcasm.

'He works very hard,' answered Elizabeth. 'But he does
a good deal at home.'

'A good deal of what? Blackie says he has some sort of
engineering firm.'

'Yes, I suppose you could call it that,' Elizabeth said,
almost as vaguely as Blackie had done. 'There was a
piece about him recently in one of the Sunday papers.
They called him one of Britain's brightest assets in the
export market. And he's not just clever, Nell. He's such
a kind, thoughtful man.' Her aunt's rather pale face glowed
and Nell looked at her curiously.

Was it possible that the cool aloof Elizabeth, whom
she never remembered showing an interest in any man,
was seriously involved with Philip? Surely she was too
old for him? And if the feeling was one-sided there could
be nothing but unhappiness ahead for her. Nell was
relieved that Elizabeth showed signs of greater friendliness
this morning. Perhaps her stiff manner yesterday had been
due more to awkwardness than to hostility. A five-year gap
in communications took time to bridge, especially as they
had never had a close relationship. Apart from her grandfather, it had been Blackie whom the child Nell had turned
to for warmth and affection.

Later that morning they drove to the hospital. Colonel

Whitehead was sufficiently recovered to be difficult, announced the Sister in charge of the intensive care unit. 'Please use your influence with him, Miss Whitehead. Make him understand he'll get better more quickly if he co-operates with us.'

'I'll do what I can,' Elizabeth said, with less self-assurance than she usually showed. 'But my father can be very obstinate.'

The understatement of the century, thought Nell, giving the sister a sympathetic smile, because she was more aware of the poor woman's problems than her non-medical aunt.

'Perhaps you could say something, Dr Ramsay?'

'I could try,' Nell agreed doubtfully, but her efforts met with total defeat.

'Don't you start telling me what to do, my girl! I detest bossy females.' The Colonel glared from his daughter to his granddaughter. 'As if I don't have enough to put up with from the nurses!'

'Now, darling, you know they're marvellous women,' soothed Elizabeth.

'Of course they're good girls, but do they have to treat me as if I was in my second childhood?' The Colonel subsided into aggrieved silence, while Sister, who had been staying tactfully in the background, moved forward and urged him not to excite himself.

'See what I mean?' the old man muttered, and Nell laid a cool hand on his forehead.

'Then the more you co-operate, Grandpa, the quicker you'll get away from them! We could nurse you at home once you're a little better.'

His eyes opened wide and his lips twitched. 'Could you really? And what about that fine career of yours? I thought it came first with you.'

'Oh, Grandpa, of course it doesn't.' Nell caught the Sister's eye. 'We'll talk about it later, when you're feeling more up to it. Right now Sister wants you to rest.'

Elizabeth went off to shop, but Nell sat on beside the old man, and presently he drifted off to sleep. His colour was better today and his face looked less pinched. As she watched beside him Nell was swept by a tide of emotion, that brought tears to her eyes. How could she have quarrelled with her grandfather? However difficult he might be, he was the man who had sat her on his knee when she was a little girl, who had kissed her better when she hurt herself, who had put her up on her first pony, who had been father and mother both to her. A warm-hearted, hot-tempered, lovable old man. Overwhelmed by a sense of guilt, she prayed passionately for his survival. If only he would get better she would give up medicine, at least for the present. Six months or a year away from a hospital needn't mean the end of her career.

Philip was as good as his word, calling in that evening at about six. Young Dr MacFarlane, whom Nell had known since her childhood, was already there. The MacFarlanes were family friends and Andrew had the evening off.

'Dad's turn for surgery,' he had announced cheerfully on his arrival. 'Thought it would be nice to catch up on your news, Nell.'

They were chatting about Queen's College Hospital, which was also Andrew's old school, and Elizabeth was knitting and not paying much attention, when the doorbell rang.

Elizabeth jumped up quickly, so that her knitting rolled on to the carpet. 'I expect that's Philip. I'll go.'

Andrew gave Nell a knowing wink. 'Dad says she's mad about him. It worries him quite a lot.'

'I wondered myself,' Nell admitted, thinking that 'mad' was too strong a word to apply to her calm, controlled aunt. 'But why should it worry him?'

'He's fond of her. I suppose he doesn't want to see her hurt.'

'You don't think Mr Trent might be interested too?'

Andrew laughed. 'Be your age! He's years younger. Well, four or five years. Rich, presentable and successful —is he likely to go for an older woman? Especially when he has hordes of gorgeous girl-friends?'

Nell had already discovered that Andrew was prone to exaggeration. A cheerful extrovert, with a round good-tempered face, he was excellent company, but she sensed that her aunt didn't entirely approve of him.

There was the murmur of voices from the hall. The others seemed in no hurry to join them, a fact which Andrew pointed out with a grin. 'Tell you what, why don't I take you to the Fox and Hounds? Leave the field clear for Elizabeth?'

The Fox and Hounds was the village pub. 'I'd like that, Andrew, but we'd better stay a few minutes or it might look rude.'

Philip greeted Andrew politely, told Nell he was delighted to hear of her grandfather's continued good progress, and accepted a whisky from Elizabeth. His manner was that of a man who was completely at home in this house. His conversation seemed a deliberate attempt to divert Elizabeth's mind from worrying about her father.

When the telephone rang they all looked at each other. Then Nell jumped up. 'Let me answer it. No reason why it should be the hospital.'

It wasn't. While Elizabeth went to talk to a friend, Philip drew his chair nearer to the fire and spoke quietly to Nell.

'Is it true that you're staying on for some time?'

'I can stay,' Nell answered cautiously, not yet convinced of her welcome, at least as far as her aunt was concerned.

A look of scorn crossed his face. 'Surely you haven't changed your mind? Elizabeth told me——'

'I'll stay if they want me to, Mr Trent.'

'Haven't you another job lined up?' asked Andrew, and she shook her head.

'I've applied for one or two—the Obstetric Unit at Q.C.H.—and another one in London, but I've heard nothing yet.'

'If you're offered the one at Queen's you musn't turn it down,' Andrew said firmly. 'You're at a crucial stage in your career, when you've just been registered. You can't afford to miss the boat.'

'I know,' Nell agreed, staring into the fire and avoiding Philip's eyes. 'I can't stay away too long, but if they want me here for a few months—if I can do anything to help——'

'A few months!' Andrew exploded. 'You'll forget everything you've learnt.'

'You don't think Nell owes anything to her family?' Philip's cool voice brought Nell's head round sharply.

'Ye-es, but in my opinion they haven't treated her particularly well. I think it's jolly decent of her to have come at all.'

'You do?' Philip's voice managed to convey both disagreement and disapproval. 'Take a bow, Nell! At least you have one champion.'

She flushed under his mocking glance. 'Let's not rake up the past, Andrew. If Elizabeth needs me——'

'She does,' Philip said softly.

'And if Grandpa wants me to stay, then of course I will. I may not be offered either of those jobs anyway. Lots of my friends have applied for them too.'

'The obstetric one must be yours for the asking,' Andrew said knowingly. 'The Prof has a weakness for pretty girls.' He gazed admiringly at Nell and nodded towards Philip. 'Never thought she'd turn out like this! Such a skinny little kid, all arms and legs. Used to tag around after me in the school holidays——'

'Oh, Andrew, do shut up!' Embarrassment made Nell revert to schoolgirl language.

'Wouldn't mind if she showed an interest now,' Andrew added, grinning broadly, and Nell gave him a cross look.

'Do stop being such an idiot! Have you had too much to drink?'

'One Scotch? Have a heart, love! Which reminds me, shall we be off?'

Nell wasn't especially keen to go out with him now, but longed to get away from Philip, who had a way of looking at her that completely destroyed her composure. It was a cold wet night, and it would have been pleasant to sit by the fire, but not in the company of Philip and her aunt.

'Can't stand that chap,' Andrew muttered as they walked to his car. 'Beats me why Dad thinks so highly of him.'

'Probably because he's rich and successful,' Nell suggested.

Andrew started up the car before replying. 'Dad's not like that. Outward show means nothing to him. It's the inner man he cares about, and I must say he's a pretty shrewd judge of character. Should be after years in our racket!'

Andrew's approach to medicine was lighthearted, at least outwardly, but that he cared about his work became apparent as the evening progressed. They moved on from the Fox and Hounds to a roadhouse, which hadn't existed when Nell left home. In these rather incongruous surroundings Andrew gave her an enthusiastic account of his plans to modernise the surgery.

'We need extra examination rooms, so that we don't have to wait ten minutes while old Mrs Muggins removes ten layers of clothes! And our equipment's out of the Ark. We need a new receptionist too! Our present one looks like Dracula!'

In between these remarks he danced with her and introduced her to several of his friends. It was past mid-

night before he brought her home, parking his car a short
distance from the front door and turning towards her.

'It's been great seeing you. We must do it again.' He
cupped her chin with his hand, turned her face towards
him and kissed her on the mouth. His breath smelt of
whisky and cigarette smoke. When he let her go Nell
moved away from him, one hand on the door. She didn't
want Andrew becoming really amorous, not outside her
aunt's bedroom windows! Not anywhere for that matter,
at least until she knew him better.

'I've enjoyed it, Andy. Thank you very much.'

As she let herself into the house she speculated with
amusement as to what Andrew must have been like as a
medical student and houseman. Mad about rugby, only
average scholastically, a great one for the nurses almost
certainly. She liked him, but found it difficult to take him
seriously, apart from his obvious enthusiasm for his work.

As she passed her aunt's door, Elizabeth called out. She
was sitting up in bed, wrapped in a pale blue bedjacket,
reading the current issue of *Vogue*. 'I couldn't settle till I
knew you were back.' A hint of reproach in the cool voice.

'Sorry, Aunt Elizabeth, but I am grown up, you know.
What did you think might happen to me?'

'With that young man, anything! He drives his M.G.
like a racing car, and Philip said he was already half drunk
when he left here.' Elizabeth removed the spectacles she
wore these days for reading, her mouth a thin line of
disapproval.

'What nonsense! Andrew knows when to stop.' Not for
anything would Nell have admitted that Andrew's style
of driving didn't exactly appeal to her either.

'Does he? I feel it's my duty to warn you that he has
a bad reputation where women are concerned. Though
knowing what modern students are like you probably
won't care.'

Nell hung on to her temper with difficulty. It would

never do to have a row so soon after returning. 'Aunt Elizabeth,' she said quietly, 'you mustn't believe everything you hear about medical students—any students for that matter. We're not all promiscuous. I shan't be hopping into bed with Andrew at the first opportunity.'

An angry flush appeared on her aunt's cheeks and crept down her neck. She looked older than her years now, prim and disapproving. 'Do you have to be so coarse? Though I suppose after all those years in medical school you're bound to become unfeminine. Philip says——'

'For goodness' sake, Aunt Elizabeth! I'm sorry, but I don't want to hear what Philip says. I'm well aware that his opinion of me isn't very high.'

Elizabeth's prim expression was replaced by a rather smug look. 'Well, you see, he prefers women who behave like women. He's such a masculine man himself, isn't he?'

'Oh, sure, if by masculine you mean overbearing and opinionated. I quite agree that he's been a good friend to you and Grandpa, but he's just not my type, Aunt Elizabeth.'

Elizabeth smiled faintly, her annoyance quite gone. 'Just as well, dear, since the feeling's mutual. And don't you think you could drop the aunt bit? As you say, you *are* grown up.'

Colonel Whitehead continued to improve, and when she wasn't visiting him, Nell travelled around the district renewing acquaintance with old friends and old haunts. Most people were pleased to see her, but a few were a little cool towards her, and these, Nell noticed, tended to be Elizabeth's friends too. Without doubt her aunt had said some very disagreeable things about her, after she had left home. Nell wondered how much her grandfather's adamant refusal to make up their quarrel had been influenced by Elizabeth's attitude.

Now he was touchingly eager to bury the past. As a

doctor she knew this was a common reaction when someone had nearly died. Such a grim reminder of mortality
made most people regret wasted time and warped relation-
ships. The Colonel liked to chat about the old days, especially when Nell was a child, and as he grew stronger the
nurses allowed him to talk more. One day, when Nell was
sitting with him, Dr Franks, who was the physician in
charge, came to see him.

'Don't run away, Dr Ramsay. Pleased with your grandfather's progress?'

'Very pleased. He looks a different man.'

'It's astonishing that I do,' grumbled the Colonel. 'That
intensive care unit was enough to frighten a man to death.
Nurses hovering over you, flicking out their syringes at the
drop of a hat! And that damned E.C.G. machine monitor-
ing every heartbeat!'

Dr Franks smiled benignly at his patient and caught
Nell's eye. 'Sure sign they're on the mend when they start
to grumble! If he behaves himself he should be ready to
go home next week. You've managed to arrange for a resident nurse?'

Nell said that she had, with the help of Dr MacFarlane
and his receptionist, who might be a dragon, but was hyper-
efficient. Outside the old man's room, Dr Franks laid a
friendly hand on her shoulder.

'Sure you can cope? That aunt of yours tends to go to
pieces in an emergency. You won't panic if he has another
coronary?'

'Might he?'

'My dear girl!' Dr Franks' face wore the pained expression that her teachers had assumed, when she gave a
particularly foolish answer on a ward round. 'You know
quite well that the risk of a second coronary is considerable,
especially at his age. He may have another, he may not, I
can't say more.'

The house physician winked at Nell behind his chief's back.

'Of course, Dr Franks. It was a silly question,' she agreed. 'I don't seem able to look at things in a detached way where my own family are concerned.'

'We're all the same, my dear.' Dr Franks patted her shoulder again. 'Doctors not only make the worst patients, they make the worst patients' relatives,' and laughing at his little joke he went off with his houseman and his registrar.

Elizabeth greeted the good news with a mixture of apprehension and pleasure. 'Well, of course I'm delighted, Nell, but what if he has a relapse?'

'Nurse Taylor will call Dr MacFarlane.'

'And if she's off duty?'

'Then I shall be around, at least until he's past the convalescent stage.'

'You won't be able to gad around so much,' Elizabeth pointed out. Why did her choice of words, and even more her way of delivering them, always imply criticism? Blackie had told Nell that the village girls rarely stayed, finding Elizabeth too much of a perfectionist, and too intent on putting them in their place when they showed a tendency towards familiarity.

'It doesn't do in this day and age,' Blackie observed, over tea in her room, an almost daily routine for them both. 'But she can't forget that she's Miss Whitehead of Lanmore Manor. Thank goodness you're not like that, Nell. It was a good thing you got away when you did.'

'Oh, Blackie, it's nice to have one person who understands. Aunt Elizabeth makes no effort, and Grandpa has only forgiven me because he's been too ill to care.'

'Not a bit of it,' Blackie said briskly. 'He'd die rather than admit it, but he's proud of you secretly. Especially now he can see for himself that you're just the same girl, in spite of your fine degree.'

Her remark reminded Nell of what Elizabeth had told her. 'Mr Trent doesn't agree, Blackie. He doesn't approve of educated women.'

'I can't believe he's so narrow-minded.'

'Aunt Elizabeth says he thinks they're unfeminine.' That conversation still rankled, and Nell coloured with annoyance.

Blackie gave a loud sniff. 'Your aunt has a habit of embroidering things. I wouldn't let it bother you. He probably said nothing of the sort. He's far too sensible.'

But Nell thought that her aunt's remarks might well be true. Philip was just the sort of man who preferred his women to be demure and malleable, decorative certainly, but most definitely not argumentative. As she tended to be in his company, she thought ruefully. Fortunately he had been away for several days at his London office, for she still found it a strain to maintain a cool composed manner when he dropped in of an evening to see Elizabeth.

A couple of days later they had an unexpected visitor— Mrs Middleton-Massey, whose daughters had been at school with Nell, and whom she had known all her life. Nell was surprised to see her, because she knew that her aunt didn't care for the other woman. Mrs Middleton-Massey made it quite plain why she had come. Striding through the hall in the old brogues she favoured, she addressed Nell in her deep, almost masculine voice.

'Glad you're back, m'dear. Been away too long.' She dropped heavily on to a dainty gold chair and submitted the girl to a searching quiz, while Elizabeth went off to organise coffee. They had reached the stage of Nell's matrimonial prospects when Elizabeth returned, and with her Philip. No whit disturbed by their arrival, Mrs Middleton-Massey continued with her catechism.

'Thank you, Elizabeth. No sugar. If I get any heavier my

horse won't be able to carry me, poor brute! So you're back, Philip? How can you bear to stay in town? Well now, Nell, as I was saying, it's high time you got yourself married. All the girls are off my hands except Pamela, thank goodness!'

'Nell is a modern girl, Roberta,' said Elizabeth with a touch of malice. 'Marriage comes fairly low on her list of priorities.'

'Nonsense, Elizabeth. All girls want to get married, even the brainy ones.' Mrs Middleton-Massey turned her small dark eyes on the unfortunate Nell, who was all too aware of Philip's ill-concealed amusement. 'Fortunately she's very presentable—yes, very presentable indeed, don't you agree, my dear man?'

'Oh, undoubtedly,' Philip returned smoothly, his face bland as he stared Nell down.

She sought, not very successfully, for a degree of composure. 'Mrs Middleton-Massey, couldn't we talk about something else? The others aren't interested in my affairs.'

Later, when Mrs Middleton-Massey was leaving, she asked Nell to walk out to the car with her. 'Wanted a few words on our own, m'dear.' She halted by the Land-Rover, drawing on serviceable string gloves. 'How are you getting on with Elizabeth, m'mm?'

'Well enough,' Nell answered cautiously.

'And that's a white lie if ever I heard one. She's no friend of yours, my girl. Never has been. Spread a lot of malicious gossip after you left.'

'Oh, please, I'd rather not hear——'

'Helps to know who one's enemies are,' the other woman said gruffly.

'Don't you think you're rather overstating the case? Aunt Elizabeth and I have never exactly been friends, but we're not *enemies*.'

'Speak for yourself, Nell. She hated your mother, so she's not likely to spare much affection for you.'

Shocked, Nell stared at Mrs Middleton-Massey. 'You can't mean that! My mother was her sister.'

'Sisters can hate each other. Jealousy usually, and your mother was always the favourite. Prettier, more affectionate, popular with young men. And such a sweet girl too. Oh yes, my dear, Elizabeth may have done her best to hide it, but she had no love for your mother, none at all.'

Her voice carried even when she was attempting too lower it, and Nell glanced over her shoulder uneasily.

'She can't hear,' boomed the other woman. 'Too taken up with that Trent fellow. And that's another thing, Nell —keep out of his way if you want a peaceful life.' At the girl's puzzled look she dug a hard forefinger into her ribs, and gave a throaty chuckle. 'He's Elizabeth's property. Surely you've noticed?'

'Oh, honestly!' Nell exploded with mirth. 'I'm not likely to compete with my aunt over him! We don't get on at all well, you know.'

'He's a man!' Mrs Middleton-Massey had a habit of stating the obvious. 'I saw the way he was looking at your legs just now!' She climbed ponderously into the Land Rover, and leant out as another thought struck her. 'You've nothing to ride now, have you? You can borrow one of the girls' horses any time you like. I kept them on after they married for old times' sake.'

Nell was delighted, for it had been a blow to discover that the stables were empty and falling into disrepair. After she left her grandfather had sold the few remaining horses, for Elizabeth had never been keen on riding, and he was too old for it.

'Goodbye, my dear,' called the older woman. 'If the wind blows too cold in this quarter you know where to come.'

She roared off in a flurry of gravel and grinding gears. A magnificent rider, she was famous for her bad driving. Dear, tactless, outrageous Mrs Middleton-Massey! Nell went back into the house, smiling, but thoughtful too. Allowing for Mrs Middleton-Massey's tendency to exaggerate, and the fact that she and Elizabeth had never been friends, there might still be a grain of truth in her remarks.

Sisters didn't always get on. They might even hate each other. Her other suggestion, that Elizabeth might come to look on Nell as a rival, was too bizarre even to contemplate.

CHAPTER THREE

COLONEL WHITEHEAD came home after the weekend, wheeled into the house in a chair with his new nurse beside him. They had converted the small sitting-room into a bedroom and Nurse Taylor, looking round with a practised eye, pronounced that it was adequate.

'Though it would have been handy to have a washbasin in the room.'

'The downstairs cloakroom's right next door,' Nell said quickly. 'His bedroom has a washbasin, but we thought he'd be happier here.'

'More in the thick of things,' agreed Nurse Taylor. 'Nicer for me too.' She patted well coiffured blonde hair, and slid her navy serge cloak from her shoulders. 'Shall I hang this in the cloakroom?' She was brisk, modern and around Elizabeth's age.

Nell thought she was ideal, mature enough to handle a difficult patient, yet not so old that she would expect to be waited on all day. Nights she was to have off except in an emergency, for Blackie had found a distant cousin, a widow, who was prepared to sit up with the Colonel.

'But if you're the least bit worried you must call me,' Nell told the woman, when she arrived that evening for her first session.

'Fuss about nothing,' grumbled Colonel Whitehead. 'Only got to ring the bell if I feel unwell, haven't I?' He glared at Blackie's cousin and the woman retreated nervously into a corner.

'Just for a week or two until we're sure you're quite out of—really on the mend,' pleaded Elizabeth.

The Colonel's bushy eyebrows drew together in an

ominous frown. 'Beginning to wish I'd stayed in hospital!
At least they had other patients to fuss over as well.'

'And here you'll get all the attention,' Nell teased him.
'You're an old fraud, Grandpa. You know you're pleased
to be home.'

The Colonel pouted his lips, so that his moustache
waggled up and down, a trick that Nell had loved as a
child. He looked round the pretty blue room, with its velvet
curtains and the brocaded day bed, at the sporting prints
on the walls that Nell had moved from his study. 'I suppose I am glad,' he conceded. 'As long as you women don't
go on at me. Too many females around, that's the trouble!'

'I'll ask Philip to look in and see you tomorrow,' Elizabeth suggested, and the old man brightened.

'I'd like that. Good lad, Philip. One of the best.'

Nell smiled to herself to hear the very adult Philip de-
scribed as a good lad, and followed Elizabeth to her grandfather's side to kiss him goodnight.

'Stay a moment, Nell. I want a word with you. Alone.'
His fierce look sent Blackie's cousin scurrying from the
room, followed more composedly by Nurse Taylor. Elizabeth lingered in the doorway.

'Nell will be along in a moment,' Colonel Whitehead
said to his daughter, and biting her lip with vexation,
Elizabeth left.

'Sit down, girl. What I have to say is important.'

'Couldn't it wait till morning? You look very tired.'

'No, it couldn't. Mightn't be here in the morning,' the
old man said bluntly. At her shocked face he added quietly,
'One has to face facts, my dear. I'm old, and if I can have
one coronary I can have another. Mind, I've every intention of getting better and plaguing you girls for years to
come!'

'Oh, Grandpa!' Swallowing on the lump in her throat,
Nell pressed his thin hand.

'Don't work yourself up, Nell. I can't stand emotional

scenes. Now what I wanted to say was, if anything happens to me, look after your aunt. She's never had to manage on her own.'

Astonished, Nell could only stare at him.

'Know just what you're thinking. That Elizabeth's fifteen years older than you, and ought to be able to look after herself. But she can't, my dear. She needs someone to lean on.'

That was possibly true, but Nell couldn't see herself as a prop to Elizabeth. However, to please her grandfather she agreed that she would always be available if she was needed.

'Will you?' he asked with a touch of wistfulness. 'You won't cut yourself off from us again?'

This wasn't the time to remind him that she had tried to make up their quarrel, that he had been the one who had been recalcitrant. 'No, Grandpa,' Nell said steadily, and she bent forward to kiss the worn old face.

Elizabeth was talking to Blackie's cousin in the hall, but moved away from her as Nell appeared. 'What did he want?' she asked sharply.

Nell didn't think her aunt would be flattered to learn that the Colonel had no opinion of his daughter's capabilities. 'Well ... nothing much. Just needed a—a bit of re-assurance.'

Elizabeth's mouth thinned in that way it had. 'Really, Nell, do you have to be so secretive? Father and I have always discussed everything.'

She swept into the drawing-room, where Nurse Taylor was already installed by the log fire and looking hopefully at the television set.

'Would you like to watch something, Sister?' Nell asked, switching on the set. Elizabeth, with an audible sigh, picked up a novel. Nell thought a little grimly that her grandfather was right. There were too many women around! Elizabeth already showed signs of disliking Nurse Taylor's bright and breezy manner. If she made it too plain they might be in trouble, for private nurses weren't easy to come by in these days, and Nurse Taylor was no shrinking violet. She would up and leave if she took offence.

Indeed it took all Nell's tact in the next few days to keep the peace. Her only opportunity to let off steam was in her visits to Blackie's room, for she was too anxious about her grandfather to go far from the house. It wasn't only his health that kept her always on hand. It was apprehension that the smouldering antagonism that had developed between Elizabeth and Nurse Taylor might break into open warfare if she wasn't around to smooth things down.

'I can't understand my aunt,' she told Dr MacFarlane on one of his morning visits. 'You'd think she'd be glad to have such competent help on the spot.'

They were alone in the library. Dr MacFarlane grunted and took a sip of the excellent sherry Nell had poured him. 'Elizabeth's a wee bit possessive over her father. Doesn't like other people doing things for him.'

'But that's absurd! She'd be grumbling she was overworked if we didn't have Nurse Taylor.'

'Of course it's absurd, but jealousy is irrational. Giving you a tough time, are they?' His shrewd eyes looked her over critically. 'You're not as bonny as you were when you came.'

'It has been a bit of a strain,' Nell admitted. 'Hard to believe I've only been home a month.'

'What you need is a day off. A complete change of scene.'

'Honestly, Dr Mac, I'm all right. Until Grandpa came home I was getting out every day.'

'And now you've been housebound for a week.' The door opened and Elizabeth came in, accompanied by Philip. 'Hallo, my dear,' said Dr Macfarlane. 'Nell was just telling me she's getting a bit jaded. Poor girl needs a break, I'm sure you'll agree.'

Nell opened her mouth to protest, but was forestalled by Elizabeth. 'Really, Sandy? No one expects her to make a martyr of herself, you know. She's free to go out when she likes.'

'Aunt Elizabeth, I don't want——'

'If you feel hard done by I wish you'd talk to me, instead of grumbling to Sandy.' Elizabeth's face was cold as she looked across at her niece.

It was useless to try and explain that she hadn't been grumbling, and that it was Dr MacFarlane who had brought up the matter, especially in front of Philip, whose very expressive face was registering open disapproval at what he probably saw as another example of her selfishness.

'Your grandfather's much better. Take tomorrow off,' urged Dr MacFarlane, who could pursue an idea doggedly when he wanted.

Irritated by her aunt's attitude and even more by Philip's unspoken criticism, Nell thought she might as well do just that. 'I believe I will,' she said. 'I'll go to London and do some shopping. Call in at the hospital and catch up on the news.' And then she remembered that she had arranged for her car to be serviced. 'Oh well, I can go another day.'

'I'll run you up,' Philip said unexpectedly. 'I have to be in the office by ten. All right?'

She wasn't too keen on the idea, but didn't see how she could turn down his offer without offence, and the inevitable unpleasantness afterwards with Elizabeth. Her aunt had already commented on the fact that Nell did her best to avoid Philip, and was no more than civil to him on the rare occasions when they did meet.

When he arrived next morning Nell was waiting in the hall, wearing her camel car coat and dark trousers. 'Wouldn't a skirt have been more suitable if you're going to the hospital?' Elizabeth asked, coming out to the car to say good morning to Philip.

'I'm only going to see my friends,' Nell said lightly, de-

termined not to let Elizabeth's old-fashioned views irritate
her today.

Philip opened the car door for her and she climbed in.
He spoke for a minute of two with Elizabeth, and Nell
caught the odd word here and there. 'These young things
are all so ...' That was Elizabeth, presumably about her.
And Philip's amused reply, 'Well, at least she's not ...'

The crunch of gravel under his feet cut off the end of
this sentence, so that Nell was left wondering about it. As
they halted at the end of the lane to let another car go by,
he turned towards her. 'Where shall I put you down? I'll
be going in through Hampstead.'

'Anywhere near your office. I can get a bus to Piccadilly.
Do my shopping first, before I go on to the hospital.'

'Wishing you were back there?' he asked, moving forward again.

His voice was neutral. She gave him a quick glance to
see if he was being disagreeable, but his face was impassive,
so she couldn't decide.

'Do I detect a note of criticism?' she asked carefully, and
he shrugged slightly and raised one hand from the wheel.

'Not really. I realise you don't have Elizabeth's sense
of family responsibility, so I suppose you've done quite well
to stick it this long.'

Nell breathed hard, but managed to control herself. 'Not
many young people do nowadays, I suppose,' he added
thoughtfully, pulled a packet of cigarettes from the glove
compartment and stuck one between his lips. 'Mind if I
smoke?'

'I don't, but you should.' Nell had recently finished six
months as a house surgeon on the Chest Unit at Q.C.H.,
and felt strongly about the risks of smoking.

'I'm not a heavy smoker.' He lit up with an expert flick
and gave her a sardonic smile. 'Haven't you any vices,
doctor?'

'Of course I have, Mr Trent. I'm selfish and self-centred.

I don't care about my family——' She broke off in con-
fusion, furious with herself for letting her tongue run away
with her. 'Isn't that what you think of me?' she added
crossly, and was even more annoyed when he laughed.

'You said it, my dear! Conscience pricking, perhaps?'

'No, it isn't. Did it ever occur to you that there are two
sides to every quarrel? And you've only heard one.'

'Spare me the petty details. I do my best not to get involved in other people's rows.'

'But you are involved!' Nell cried indignantly. 'You've
made it plain ever since we met that you're on Elizabeth's
side.'

'I'm not on anyone's side.' He sounded bored and contemptuous. 'Don't you think it's time you grew up, and
stopped being such a trial to your unfortunate family?'

Nell was so angry that she nearly told him to stop the car.
However, a moment's reflection made her realise that she
was some way from a bus stop and she didn't fancy hitch-
ing a lift. So she swallowed hard, stared out of the window
and waited until she had herself under control. 'I don't
want to discuss family affairs either, Mr Trent,' she managed in a cool little voice, since she was quite unable to
think of anything more cutting to say.

'Good grief, my dear girl, do you think I do?' he exclaimed, and after that they were silent, which was at least
better than arguing.

She thanked him stiffly when he swung into a side road
behind Oxford Street.

'Want a lift back? You could meet me at my office.'

'No, thank you. I'm not sure what time I'll be leaving.'

He walked round the car to open her door. 'It's up to
you. If you change your mind give me a ring. Trent Electronics—it's in the yellow pages.'

She looked up at him in some indignation. 'I can't understand you, Mr Trent.'

'Philip. Now what's bothering you?'

'We did nothing but argue all the way up——'

'Except when you sat in smouldering silence!'

'Yes, well—surely you can't want my company on the return journey?'

His sudden grin made him look years younger. 'I can bear it if you can. It's up to you, Nell.' He raised a hand in farewell and turned away.

Nell was delighted to catch up with all the hospital gossip. When she had finished her shopping she called in at the residents' mess and had lunch with her friends. They were all there, Belinda and Jimmy and Ted, long back from Switzerland, but still tanned and fit-looking. Beside them she felt pale and unattractive.

'So how much longer are you going to be stuck down there?' asked Ted towards the end of the meal, and Nell gave a sigh.

'I wish I knew. It depends how Grandpa does.'

'Have you heard about the obstetric job yet?'

'No. Still waiting.'

Belinda and Ted were doing another six months at Q.C.H. Jimmy Green, to Belinda's sorrow, was moving out of London. 'Only thirty miles away,' he said bracingly. 'We'll still be able to see each other, Belle.'

'But not so often,' wailed Belinda, who was very much in love. 'I shall feel green with jealousy every time I think of all those nurses, looking for an unattached houseman.'

Jimmy's smile was warming. 'But I'm not unattached, love. Come on, don't you trust me?'

When the men had gone the two girls sat on, alone, for Belinda had no special duties on that afternoon. 'Only clerking new patients. I can do that later.' She seemed moody and unsettled.

'Is it just because Jimmy's going?' asked Nell.

Belinda nodded. 'I know it's silly, but I'm mad about the man. Aren't you missing Ted?'

'Oh, Belinda, that's different. Ted and I are not in love.'

'Speak for yourself,' said Belinda seriously. 'Ted hasn't been himself since you went away.'

Nell found this remark disquieting. A kind girl, she didn't what to hurt Ted, whom she liked enormously, but she realised now that she had scarcely thought about him while she was in Shropshire. He had asked her to meet him later, for he had a few hours off duty that evening. 'I'm not dressed for gadding,' she had said doubtfully, and he had answered firmly,

'We're not going on the town. I just want to talk.'

She wasn't looking forward to the evening. She didn't want Ted getting intense and demanding. He took her to a pub in the Baker Street area and bought her sandwiches and a glass of cider. Even after her years at medical school Nell had never acquired a taste for beer.

'I've missed you very much, Nell.' They were ensconced in a corner, near to a radiator, and Ted's face was flushed, but whether from heat or emotion it was difficult to say.

Nell wriggled out of her coat and made a business of hanging it over the back of her chair. 'Have you, Ted?' She tried for a light tone. 'With all those pretty nurses around?'

'Don't be flip, Nell. You know how I feel about you.'

He leant forward and put a large hand over hers. A lock of fair hair fell into his eyes and he brushed it back impatiently. 'I'm in love with you—have been for ages.'

'Oh, Ted, I don't know what to say!'

They stared intently at each other, Nell distressed, Ted with a brave attempt at cheerfulness. 'O.K., my love, I understand. But I'm still hoping. You do like me?'

'Oh, Ted,' said Nell for the second time, less articulate than usual, and that was the moment that two men seated themselves at the vacant table nearby. She saw them out of the corner of her eye, but didn't take in their faces.

'I have a free weekend in ten days' time. I could come down to see you.' Ted looked sideways at the next table and then back at Nell. 'Why's that character staring at you?' he asked under his breath. 'Do you know him?'

Nell turned her head and found herself looking into Philip Trent's grey eyes, only a few feet away from her own. She was at once overcome with self-consciousness, because Ted still had hold of her hand.

'Small world,' Philip said pleasantly. Nell tugged her hand away and Philip smiled. 'Sorry to interrupt. Aren't you going to introduce me?'

Ted's boyish face was registering open annoyance. He looked young and gauche, and Nell felt a flash of irritation that he couldn't match up to the easy manners of the older man. Philip was introducing them both to his companion.

'My partner, James Fenton.'

Mr Fenton was older than Philip, a serious-looking man with a dry manner. They made polite conversation for a minute or two, then Ted said it was time to go.

'Don't let us drive you away, my dear chap,' murmured Philip. 'We're going back to the office shortly.'

Ungraciously Ted muttered that they hadn't intended staying, and to cover an awkward moment Nell commented on the long hours Philip worked.

He shrugged. 'James and I aren't nine-to-five types. We work until we're finished. The office is just around the corner. Sure you don't want that lift?'

Ted was helping Nell on with her coat. He put a possessive arm round her shoulders and reminded her that she was coming back to the hospital with him. Nell wasn't keen on this idea, but couldn't shame him by refusing in front of the other men.

'Staying the night?' Philip asked, and she shook her head quickly.

'Catching the last train.'

In the end she caught an earlier one because her evening with Ted ended disagreeably. On the way back to the hospital he insisted on questioning her about Philip. Who was that chap? How long had she known him? When he heard that she had come to town with Philip his jealousy became open. In the privacy of his room in the residents' quarters, he lectured her on getting involved with a smooth character like Trent.

'He's far too old for you. Don't encourage him.'

Nell was losing patience fast. 'Do stop being so silly! All the man did was give me a lift, because my car was out of action. He doesn't approve of me, and I certainly don't like him.'

'He wasn't looking at you as if he disapproved of you,' Ted said obstinately. 'I hate the thought of him being your next-door neighbour.'

'So do I!'

'I'll bet! Girls always go for older men,' he said glumly. 'Now if only he looked like that stick of a partner——'

'I should probably like him more,' said Nell, attempting a joke, 'then you really would have to worry.'

Ted gave her a disbelieving scowl. 'You know perfectly well Trent's ten times better looking than that other chap. I'm not a fool. Those dark forceful types are always popular with girls.'

'Not this girl,' Nell said firmly, but when he refused to be convinced she said they might as well go down to the common-room, and shortly after that she left.

Sitting in the train, she brooded over the unfortunate chance that had made Philip and his partner walk into just that pub. Or fortunate perhaps, because as a result of her disagreement with Ted she had been able to leave earlier than she might otherwise have done. This reflection made her feel rather mean, but Ted's new air of possessiveness was becoming decidedly irritating.

At the station she telephoned her aunt, and asked to be picked up. 'Sorry to be a nuisance, but I've tried in vain for a cab.'

Elizabeth said she would be there as soon as possible,

but it was Philip's blue Aston Martin that drew up by the station entrance fifteen minutes later.

'Your aunt's rather tired,' he said briefly as he slung Nell's purchases on the back seat, thereby making her feel that she was being a thorough nuisance.

When she apologised he shrugged and started the car. 'If you'd come on the last train it would have been worse. Were you expecting Elizabeth to meet that?'

'I thought I'd be able to pick up a taxi. One usually can.'

He asked her why she'd changed her mind. 'I thought you were all set for an evening with the boy-friend.'

'Well, you thought wrong.' Why did he always bring out the worst in her, making her ill-mannered and aggressive? He had after all put himself out to meet her, for the station was seven miles from Lanmore. 'I didn't feel like a late night after all,' she amended in a more conciliatory tone. 'And you've got it all wrong. Ted's not my boy-friend. Just a—a chap I've known for years.'

'You could have fooled me,' Philip remarked. 'When we came into that pub you were holding hands and gazing into each other's eyes very intently. I felt quite embarrassed at interrupting you.'

'I don't believe you,' said Nell crossly, remembering his expression when she first saw him—amused, mocking, not in the least embarrassed. 'And we were not holding hands. At least I wasn't—oh, what's the use? You aren't interested.'

'Not very,' he agreed negligently, and put his foot down on the accelerator. When they reached the house he said he wouldn't come in again. He had only called in to tell Elizabeth he would meet the late train.

Nell stared at him. 'You mean to meet me? That—that was kind of you, Philip, though it might not have been necessary.'

'It turned out to be necessary,' he pointed out. 'And I didn't want Elizabeth having to go out. You must have noticed that she's looking far from well.'

Sensing criticism that she should jaunt off to London, leaving her aunt to manage, Nell said rather stiffly that she hadn't noticed it. Elizabeth looked just the same as usual to her.

He made an exasperated sound and flicked the interior light on. 'I don't understand you, my girl. Your aunt brought you up and made considerable sacrifices for you. Don't you feel any affection for her at all?'

'Correction—Grandpa brought me up. And Blackie. Aunt Elizabeth doesn't like kids. Surely you've noticed, if you know her so well?'

She regretted this speech as soon as she had made it, and fumbled for the door handle, wanting only to get away from him. His hand shot out, restraining her. When he spoke his voice was scornful.

'What a malicious little bitch you are! Elizabeth's entirely right. She has a lot to put up with, poor woman.'

The unfairness of this attack brought tears of exasperation to Nell's eyes. So Elizabeth grumbled about her to Philip, hinted at sacrifices made on her niece's behalf. If anyone had given up time to the child Nell, it had been Blackie, not her cool remote aunt. However, it was useless trying to convince him of this. He was too firmly on Elizabeth's side, too convinced of Nell's lack of gratitude.

'Would you please let me go, Mr Trent,' she said in a low, furious voice, and as his grip slackened she jerked her hand away and flung the door open.

She was badly upset by this unpleasant scene, and would have preferred to slip into her bedroom unnoticed. Elizabeth's door was ajar, however, and she called out as Nell passed. Reluctantly the girl stopped. 'Do you want something, Elizabeth?' Her voice was cold and Elizabeth put on her spectacles to study her.

'Just to say goodnight. I hope you thanked Philip for his kindness in collecting you.'

Her manner was that of a bossy adult to a young child. Nell laughed in spite of herself, but it was an angry laugh and Elizabeth stared at her. 'Is something wrong? You look upset.'

'No, no! I'm not a bit upset!' Nell exclaimed with sarcasm. 'I like being told I'm ungrateful and uncharitable. What exactly have you said to Philip about me, to make him so disapproving?'

The other woman went pink. 'I don't know what you're talking about. Naturally, since Philip's a good friend, he knows how you've behaved. I hope you haven't been rude to him.'

'No ruder than he was to me. He called me a malicious little bitch. Charming, don't you think?'

Elizabeth took off her spectacles again and began to undo her bedjacket. 'Why do you have to quarrel with Philip when he's been so kind to us? You've upset me very much.' She put a hand to her forehead and shut her eyes.

Nell studied her aunt's face, which certainly looked pale without make-up. 'He said you aren't well. Is that true?'

Elizabeth opened her eyes again and Nell was struck by the dark shadows under them. 'I've got a headache. I get them lately.'

'Perhaps you need your specs changing?'

'No, Nell. I get headaches when I'm upset. And you don't help by being difficult. I'm tired now. I want to go to sleep.'

Dismissed, Nell went slowly away, wishing she understood Elizabeth better. Her aunt looked a lot older when she had creamed the make-up off her face. Had she had a hard time, living with the old man? Had he been difficult and demanding? If so Elizabeth would have had to bear the brunt of it with herself away. Was that why her aunt resented her so much, or was there some truth in Mrs Middleton-Massey's assertions?

As she undressed Nell thought wistfully of the wider

world of medicine, which she was beginning to miss very
badly. Domestic life, with all its trivial irritations and
jealousies, wasn't for her, at least not yet, while she was in
her early twenties. She supposed it was different when you
were in love, though most of her women friends who got
married managed to combine domesticity and a career very
successfully.

Andrew MacFarlane came to see Colonel Whitehead two
days later, since Thursday was his father's day off. 'We have
a whole day each, once a week,' he told Nell, when she
walked to the car with him at the end of his visit. 'And
alternate weekends. We need the time off if we're to stay
sane, but the days when we're single-handed are pretty
tough.'

He wasn't grumbling, just stating a fact. Country G.P.s
in small practices worked far harder than their city colleagues. 'You look jolly well on it. Andrew,' Nell smiled, but
she remembered that his father, who had called yesterday,
had looked quite grey with tiredness. It was then that she
had an idea. 'I'm going bonkers hanging around the house.
How would it be if I helped out in the practice occasionally? Just for something to do. I wouldn't expect to get
paid.'

Andrew had the car door open, but he shut it again, his
face lighting up. 'It's a great idea, Nell! Dad and I are hard
pressed, with all that new building in the village. We've
been talking about an assistant for some time, but it hasn't
yet been approved by the Executive Council.'

'Well then ... do say yes. I'd love to do it.'

'I'll have to talk to Dad, but if he agrees I know he'll
insist on paying you at the going rate.' He took a step for-
wards, put an arm round her shoulders and planted a kiss
on her cheek. 'I'll make Dad agree,' he promised. 'It's just
what we need.'

His father approved wholeheartedly of the idea. Next morning, when he had completed his examination of the Colonel, he told Nell that he wanted a word with her. Elizabeth accompanied them into the library and insisted on sitting him down by the fire with a sherry.

'Well now, my dear'—Dr Mac smiled across at Nell, who stood expectantly by the mantelpiece—'Andrew's told me what you discussed, and I think it's an excellent idea.'

She was delighted. 'How soon can I start? How much do you want me to do?'

Her aunt, who was sitting beside the doctor, looked from one to the other. 'What's this, Sandy? Is Nell going to work for you?'

He showed surprise. 'Haven't you told Elizabeth, my dear?'

'It was only an idea,' Nell said quickly, and Elizabeth added coolly,

'I'm the last person she'd tell.'

'I wish you wouldn't talk like that,' Nell sighed, wondering why her aunt always felt this unpleasant urge to snipe at her.

Dr Mac cleared his throat. 'Well now! To get down to business. How much are you prepared to do? And how much can Elizabeth spare you?'

'I can do as much as you want!' exclaimed Nell eagerly, but seeing the disapproval on Elizabeth's face added an amendment. 'Provided it doesn't clash with the times I'm needed here.'

They worked out a possible timetable, with which Elizabeth grudgingly agreed. Evening surgeries on Tuesdays and Thursdays, so that the man on his own would have at least two hours off in the twenty-four, Wednesday morning because it was always a busy one, and Saturday morning because whoever was on for the weekend usually had a heavy round of visits on that day.

'Four surgeries. Enough to keep you out of mischief!'
the doctor commented briskly, finished his sherry, thanked
Elizabeth for her hospitality and made for the door,

'Enough to keep my hand in too,' Nell said happily, almost skipping along beside him, so glad was she to be
starting work again.

Elizabeth had gone off somewhere and there was nobody
else around. Dr MacFarlane looked down at Nell's bright
face, took her by the arm and led her outside.

'Understand, my dear, this is just a friendly arrangement. If it's not always possible for you to come you only
have to let us know.'

'I shall make sure it is possible,' she assured him.

'Your aunt might need you. Or your grandfather.'

'It's only four sessions a week. Why should they, except
in an emergency? And Grandpa is getting better.'

'I was thinking more of Elizabeth's needs,' Dr MacFarlane
said with a touch of dryness. 'Why do you two get on so
badly, Nell?'

'Is it that obvious?'

'I'm afraid it is. Elizabeth was hurt just now that you
hadn't confided in her. Couldn't you be a little more ...
tactful?'

'I do try, Dr Mac. Honestly.' Nell stared at him with
troubled eyes. 'But she doesn't exactly meet me half way.'

'Elizabeth is at a difficult time in a woman's life, on the
threshold of the forties. She's seen her chance of marriage
slipping away, while she's stayed at home to look after your
grandfather.'

Nell didn't think that her very choosy aunt had ever met
a man she had wanted to marry, or that staying at home
and being Miss Whitehead of Lanmore Manor had been
so disagreeable a life. She remembered Elizabeth as being
much involved in the social life of the district, a keen
churchwoman, a leading light in the Women's Institute, with
a wide circle of friends. Her life had always been varied and

interesting. It was only now, since her father's illness, that her social activities had had to be curtailed.

Of course she said none of this to Dr MacFarlane, because it would have sounded ungenerous. Instead she told him that she would encourage Elizabeth to get out more. 'Perhaps being at home so much is making her irritable.'

'More than likely,' agreed Dr Mac, his shrewd eyes crinkling at the corners as he smiled at her. 'As your grandfather says, there are just too many females in this house!'

CHAPTER FOUR

NELL started work next Wednesday morning, arriving at the surgery before Andrew, so eager was she to begin. She introduced herself to Miss Winter, whom Andrew had likened to Dracula. Not a fair comparison. Miss Winter might look fierce, and could certainly put cheeky patients in their place, but she welcomed Nell warmly, saying it was high time her doctors had a bit of help.

Andrew's greeting was just as enthusiastic, and Nell felt a glow of pleasure at getting back to work in such congenial surroundings. Andrew sorted through the thick pile of case notes, giving her the ones he thought would be easiest.

'Mrs Willis and Mrs Burton—both hypochondriacs. They're here for a chat. And old Mr Davies. He'd love to see a pretty girl! And all three of the Crawford children, my God! I don't suppose they've anything serious. Coughs and colds probably—their mother's a chronic worrier.'

'Can't I have anyone interesting?' Nell queried ruefully, and he patted her shoulder encouragingly.

'Breaking you in gradually. And letting you see what a G.P.'s life is really like. Ninety per cent trivial complaints, ten per cent serious!'

However, the trivial complaints mattered to the people who had them, though they were often only an excuse to come to the surgery. Unhappiness, loneliness and boredom weren't diseases, but they could lead to ill health. Andrew talked about this when they had coffee together at the end of the surgery.

'Old people are the worst sufferers in modern society. Often they're entirely cut off from their families, either through distance or lack of interest. I went to India once as a student, and they can teach us a lot about family life, for all our assumption of Western superiority.'

Miss Winter, who had been a dispenser in a mission hospital, agreed with him entirely. 'They don't condemn their old folk to life in a Home or a bed-sitter, as we so often do. Did you manage all right, Dr Ramsay? Could you read Dr Andrew's writing?'

Miss Winter was a privileged person and allowed to tease her doctors. Nell smiled at her and agreed that Andrew's writing was atrocious. Even worse than his father's!

She drove back to the Manor in a glow of satisfaction, pleasure at being back at work, and relief that she had coped quite adequately. Andrew had been pleased with her and had said that before long she could take surgeries on her own.

'Then Dad or I can start visits earlier. This time of year there's always a long list.'

It was already the beginning of March, dull blustery days with scarcely a gleam of sunshine. When Nell had been at home most of the time she had found the gloomy weather depressing. Now she sang as she drove through the narrow country lanes. Her exhilaration was a little damped when she arrived home to find Philip's car near the front door. She hadn't seen him for over a week, not since that evening when he had brought her back from the station. Blackie had mentioned that he was away.

'He comes and goes a lot. Stays in his London flat some weeks, travels abroad a great deal.'

'Portrait of a successful globe-trotting business man,' Nell had commented, and Blackie had looked at her in surprise.

'Don't you like him? I think he's a real gentleman.'

Nell parked behind Philip's car and went slowly into the house. Remembering her last meeting with him, she felt some embarrassement, but was determined not to show it.

They were all in the library, the Colonel, her aunt and Philip, Nurse Taylor and Blackie too, the women with glasses of sherry, the men drinking whisky. It was unusual for Blackie to join in like this.

'What's up?' asked Nell. 'Is this a celebration?'

Her grandfather beamed at her. 'Yes indeed. Dr Franks called this morning. He says I can do more now—join the rest of the family for meals, go for short walks with Nurse Taylor.'

'That's wonderful!' Nell crossed the room and stooped to kiss the old man's cheek. As she straightened she met Philip's eyes. 'Hallo,' she said coolly, and he inclined his head slightly in return.

'Pour Nell a drink, please, Philip,' said her grandfather.

Philip moved towards the drinks cupboard, turned and asked her what she wanted. The others were talking. Philip's mouth turned up at the corners, but not in a proper smile.

'Not pleased with me?' he murmured. 'In view of the occasion do you think you could hide it?'

She almost snatched the glass from his hand. 'I thought I had. No one else seemed to notice.'

'They're too taken up with the old man's good news. Do you think he'll make a complete recovery?'

'Hard to say. He's over seventy.'

'And does this mean you'll be returning to London soon——'

'I don't think so. Not for another month or two anyway.'

The smile was a real one now, softening his rather hard face, so that even Nell, who didn't like him, was aware of his attraction. She blinked and moved away from him, joining her grandfather by the fire. The Colonel asked how she had got on that morning. To everyone's surprise he had accepted the fact of her working with complete lack of argument.

'Shouldn't think the men were too pleased, having to see a chit of a girl,' he remarked, eyes glinting beneath bushy eyebrows.

Nell took this correctly as a heavy-handed attempt at a joke, and answered in kind. 'As a matter of fact they loved it. One old man booked his next visit on my day. I heard him asking Miss Winter if he could see me.'

'Old fool,' rumbled Colonel Whitehead, and Philip, strolling across to join them, gave Nell an amused look.

'Work certainly seems to agree with you. You're positively sparkling today.'

'Glad to get away from us,' Elizabeth said sourly. 'You know how easily she gets bored.'

Nell flushed. 'No, I don't. It's just that—that I'm trained for a certain job, and it seems such a waste not to use my training!'

Unexpectedly Philip agreed with her. 'It's always a pity when someone wastes their skills. Seems the ideal solution to me. The MacFarlanes are hard pressed and Nell wants to work.' He smiled at her again, as warmly as before, and Nell's hand tightened on her glass.

It was extraordinary how pleasant he was being today, as if he was making a deliberate effort to charm her. And almost succeeding, she thought ruefully, staring at him as he stood by the fireplace, tall, well built, ruggedly handsome.

Blackie disappeared into the kitchen and a few minutes later the lunch gong sounded from the hall. Elizabeth gave the Colonel her arm, fussing over the old man in a way that plainly irritated him. As father and daughter went out of the room Nell hung back for a second, and spoke to Philip.

'Why the sudden approval?' she asked.

His eyebrows went up. 'Don't fancy me as an ally?'

'I'm wondering what's behind it.'

He took her by the arm and marched her towards the door. 'What a suspicious girl you are! Do you enjoy quarrelling with people?'

She pulled her arm away, pausing for a moment to look up at him. 'Not really.' She smiled a little uncertainly. 'I suppose it would be more ... civilised ... if we could get on.'

'I agree with you,' he said solemnly, so that she suspected mockery and gave him a doubtful look. His face, when he chose it, gave little away, so that she was left wondering why his behaviour had changed so markedly. He couldn't have forgotten the rude names he had called her in the car. *She* most certainly hadn't, Nell thought indignantly, as she seated herself at the lunch table. She was still puzzling about it when the others' conversation intruded on her thoughts.

'We'd love to have lunch with you, Philip,' her aunt was saying, 'but perhaps this Sunday is a bit soon for Father. Could we come the following one instead?'

'Easter Sunday? Certainly,' Philip agreed, and Elizabeth gave him an affectionate look.

'It'll be like old times again.'

'Old times?' Nell enquired, and her aunt explained.

'We've been having Sunday lunch with Philip for years now.'

'But—but why?' She stared from one to the other of them, surprised, not for the first time, by the degree of intimacy that had sprung up between Philip and her family.

'Why?' Philip repeated. 'Because we enjoy each other's company, of course.'

'And Sunday was such a lonely day with just the two of us in this big house,' sighed Elizabeth, giving her niece a reproachful look.

Nell flushed and bit her lip. Elizabeth lost no opportunity for digs like that. Now she was speaking to Philip again. 'You don't mind if we bring Nell?' There was a hint of apology in her voice as if she regretted having to make this request.

Before Philip could answer Nell stepped in, her colour heightened. 'It's all right, Aunt Elizabeth. I'll stay at home with Blackie.'

Everyone looked surprised and Blackie reminded Nell that she was going to be away for Easter, having a short holiday with her sister.

'My dear Nell,' said Philip in a kindly, avuncular manner that made her want to throw something at him, 'I assure you you'll be most welcome. There'll be a house full for Easter. One more will make no difference.'

After lunch Nell helped Blackie with the dishes. She was still brooding over Philip's invitation, and told the older woman that she would just as soon go up to Q.C.H. for the day.

'Don't be difficult, Nell!' Blackie spoke with unusual sharpness. 'It will look so rude if you refuse to go.'

'I suppose so,' Nell agreed reluctantly. She frowned over the wine glass she was polishing, and Blackie told her to be careful.

'You'll break the stem if you go on like that. And what's wrong with going to Mr Trent's house? They say he's a wonderful host.'

'He can afford to be, with all that money,' Nell snapped, and Blackie swished the suds vigorously.

'My, my, you're in a bad mood today! Just what is it about poor Mr Trent that upsets you so much?'

'Good question,' Nell said, but she wasn't sure of the answer. Perhaps, she thought, it was because, even when he was being pleasant, he treated her as if she was a little girl. To a fully fledged young woman doctor that was more than just irritating. It was downright insulting.

The one place where she *was* treated as an adult was at the surgery. She looked forward to her sessions there with

enthusiasm, gave of her best to the patients, and wrote
meticulous notes in her small neat hand.

'Putting Dad and me to shame,' said Andrew jokingly,
as he sifted through the list of patients who needed home
visits. 'In a hurry to get back, Nell? If you're not, care to
come round with me?'

She was delighted at the idea. 'That would be fun,
Andrew.'

Andrew smiled at her eager face and winked at Miss
Winter. 'Fun! When she's been at it a few more years she'll
change her tune.'

'I don't think she will,' Miss Winter disagreed. The
daughter and granddaughter of a doctor, she spoke with
some authority. 'Dr Ramsay has a real gift for medicine. I
can always tell.'

'Isn't Miss Winter sweet?' Nell enthused as she climbed
into Andrew's car.

He made a droll face. 'Sweet is not the word I'd apply to
the old battleaxe, but she's certainly taken a fancy to you.
We all have for that matter. We'll miss you when you go
back to London.'

'I'm in no hurry,' Nell told him, and found to her surprise that it was true. After years of living in student hostels
or bedsitters in the back streets of London, it was heartwarming to live in her old home again, firmly re-entrenched
in her grandfather's affection. If Elizabeth's tongue was still
sharp, Nell could laugh it off more easily, now that she had
the outlet of her work.

Their last visit took them down a familiar road. 'Mrs
Middleton-Massey lives just round the bend,' Nell remarked, and Andrew smiled.

'So she does. Haven't seen the old girl lately.'

'Have we time to look in? Just for a few minutes?'

The Middleton-Masseys were the most hospitable
people for miles and were always delighted when they had
unexpected visitors. Five minutes later Nell and Andrew

were seated in their drawing-room with drinks in front of them, listening to Mr Middleton-Massey's account of his most recent hunting misfortune. A wiry man of only medium height, he made a curious contrast to his large wife, but if casual acquaintances found them comical, Nell knew better. How wonderful to be so happily married, she thought. They were too contented and too busy to have time for the minor ailments of middle age.

Archie,' Mrs Middleton-Massey boomed, 'fill Andrew's glass up, m'dear.'

Andrew shook his head. 'I'm on duty, but Nell isn't.'

Nell was a light drinker. She put her hand over her glass. 'None for me either. I suppose we should be going.'

'Not before I've heard how you're getting on. Your grandfather and Elizabeth treating you properly?'

'Yes, of course.'

'No of course about it, my girl. Had a long talk with Philip Trent last weekend,' Mrs Middleton-Massey added with seeming inconsequence. Puzzled by her remark, Nell remained silent. 'About you, m'dear.'

Andrew was getting restive, glancing at his watch. The men went out, followed more slowly by the two women. 'I hope he didn't convert you to his point of view,' Nell joked. 'He doesn't approve of me, you know.'

Mrs Middleton-Massey poked her with a hard forefinger. 'Quite the contrary. *I* converted him. Told him a few home truths about Elizabeth.'

'Wasn't that rather tactless? They're very good friends.'

'Probably was, but Archie says tact has never been one of my strong points. Especially when I see an injustice be-ing done.' She gave Nell a sly smile. 'Anyway, even if I didn't change his mind completely I gave him food for thought.'

The idea of Philip and Mrs Middleton-Massey mulling over her affairs didn't appeal to Nell. The trouble about living in the country was that everybody knew everybody else's business, though after the anonymity of city life, even that might not be a such a bad thing.

The days flew by, with Colonel Whitehead maintaining a steady improvement. Every morning he stumped along the drive, armed with a shooting stick, on to which he would subside when he felt tired. Elizabeth was fully occupied with W.I. affairs and plans to make this Easter's church decorations the best in living memory. Nell was getting on better with her aunt, chiefly because they saw so little of each other, except at meals. Her grandfather was inclined to grumble, saying that they had no time for him. Now that Nurse Taylor was gone, he would be thoroughly bored if Philip didn't drop in occasionally for the odd game of chess.

'Grandpa, you're a shocking fraud,' Nell reproved lovingly. 'When Nurse Taylor was here you couldn't wait to get rid of her. And I haven't been out for nights.'

'Just as well,' grunted the old man. 'That lad keeps you out far too late.'

The lad was Andrew, whom Nell was having some difficulty in controlling. She enjoyed his company, but deplored his tendency to think that every girl he took out was eager for lovemaking. After their last date Nell had vowed that she wouldn't go out with him again. Andrew had grinned in his goodhumoured way and promised to behave, but thought he acted circumspectly enough at the surgery, he had a way of looking at her that made Nell blush.

It was Andrew's behaviour that caused Nell to hesitate over a proposal put to her by old Dr MacFarlane. 'The local Health Executive have at last passed our request for an assistant,' he told her one day, and the girl knew a sudden stab of disappointment.

'So I shan't be needed much longer?' she queried regretfully. 'Have you advertised the job already?'

'No, my dear.' Dr MacFarlane smiled across at his son,

who lounged against the corner of his father's desk. 'Andrew and I are wondering if you might be interested You fit in so well. We should be delighted to have you. Assistant with a view, as they say.'

That meant with a view to partnership. 'I'm flattered,' smiled Nell, 'but I haven't really finished my training. I've only done jobs in general medicine and surgery. I'd thought of obstetrics next, then perhaps paediatrics and geriatrics.'

'Not absolutely necessary,' observed Dr MacFarlane. 'You've already picked up a lot in the practice, and you could always have time off for study leave ... or to go on courses. And if you have problems we're here to consult.'

It was tempting. Nell had discovered a real liking for general practice, and wondered why so many of her friends regarded it as the last resort if they failed to make the grade in the hospital career structure.

'I'll think about it,' she promised, and that night in bed she mulled over the problem. She enjoyed the work, she liked the MacFarlanes, and surely her grandfather would be pleased? Elizabeth she couldn't answer for, though her aunt had certainly made a real effort to be more friendly lately. Andrew? If she made it plain that she would never think of him as more than a friend, surely he would have the sense to behave? She decided to telephone tomorrow and ask Belinda's advice.

Belinda was vehemently against the idea. 'Don't bury yourself in the country. You're a very bright girl, you could go right to the top.'

'I'm not sure I want to,' Nell said doubtfully. 'I don't see myself as a pushy registrar, competing in the teaching hospital rat-race.'

'You won't have to,' Belinda said with a giggle. 'You're one of the lucky ones, girl. Brainy *and* beautiful. It helps, believe me.' There was not a trace of envy in her voice. Belinda was a good friend, and besides, she had Jimmy Green, to whom she was now engaged. 'Ted's here,' she added. 'Talk it over with him.'

'Ted won't be interested,' Nell said quickly. There had been no communication between them since her visit to London.

'Of course he will.' There was a murmur of voices the other end and Ted came on the line.

'Hallo, Nell.' He sounded a little awkward. 'What's this about you going into general practice?'

'Just an idea. Nothing's definite yet.'

'Keep it that way. You'd be crazy to accept. This is where the action is,' said Ted, sounding more himself now.

'I'm not sure you're right. I think the important action is right here in general practice, and not in the teaching hospitals.'

'They've corrupted you down there,' joked Ted, and then more seriously, 'Don't do anything in a hurry, Nell.' He lowered his voice. 'Know something? I miss you very much.'

'I miss you all too,' Nell answered, and he sighed.

'Not quite the same thing. When are you coming up again?'

'We're pretty busy just now. Not before Easter.'

'Then I'll have to come down,' Ted said firmly, and though Nell had some doubts about that, she hadn't the heart to discourage him.

CHAPTER FIVE

By the time Easter arrived Nell was surprised to find that she was quite looking forward to visiting Philip's house. If she wasn't exactly on friendly terms with him at least they were no longer antagonists. On the few occasions when they had met lately, they had got on fairly well, though Nell never felt entirely at ease with him. He was too big, too masculine, too sure of himself. He made her feel inadequate, and that was something she hadn't experienced since her schooldays.

However, she had heard so much about Philip's house that she was curious to see it for herself. Blackie was always extolling its virtues compared with the old-fashioned manor which she had to run, and on Good Friday she was still on this theme. 'Your grandfather has been saying for years that he intends to modernise this place.' Blackie waved a disparaging hand round the shabby kitchen.

'I like it this way,' Nell protested, 'and so do the dogs!' She stooped to tickle Paddy behind the ears, where he lay on the worn old rug in front of the stove, revelling in its gentle warmth.

'You wouldn't if you had to work in it,' Blackie said sourly, and at Nell's distressed look, 'I'm getting on, dearie. I've reached an age when I could do with things a bit easier. And when I give up no one else will be prepared to work under these conditions.'

'Oh, Blackie, we couldn't manage without you!'

'Some day you'll have to. Or move to a smaller place. Times have changed, Nell, though your family don't seem able to accept it.'

This was near heresy from one of Blackie's conservative

disposition. Was it a warning? A hint that they had all been selfish, relying on her undoubted loyalty to the family, and forgetting that she was nearly seventy.

Nell determined to bring this conversation up with her aunt and her grandfather at the first opportunity. After Blackie had been driven off by her brother-in-law for a richly deserved break she looked for Elizabeth, but couldn't find her.

On Easter morning the family went to church, before going on to Philip's for lunch. Colonel Whitehead's only concession to his recent illness was that he had given up reading the lessons. Archie Middleton-Massey did this instead, but his voice didn't carry as well as her grandfather's, and Nell's attention wandered during the second lesson. She gazed round the lovely old Norman church, where so many of her ancestors were buried, at the exquisite rose window, which was internationally famous, at the magnificent carved reredos, and at all the old friends in the congregation, who had begun to accept her as one of themselves again.

'This is where I belong,' she thought. 'Here in Lanmore.' She was almost sure then that she would accept Dr Mac-Farlane's offer.

Half the congregation seemed to be going to Philip's house. 'Not all for lunch, surely?' Nell asked, as they crossed the cattle grid at the top of his drive.

'Good gracious, no! Only his close friends will be staying for lunch,' Elizabeth answered complacently. 'But he's asked quite a crowd in for drinks.'

Once it had been her grandfather who was the accepted leader of local society. When Nell commented on this the old man turned to smile at her from his seat in the front of the car. 'I can't be bothered with entertaining these days, and Elizabeth enjoys going to Philip's place.'

Nell gazed out of the window at the well kept drive and the immaculate lawns that lay beyond, at the modern house which harmonised so well with its surroundings. Stone seemed to mellow quicker than brick and its walls were already covered by a variety of climbing plants. They parked behind the Middleton-Masseys' Land-Rover, and found Philip at the door, waiting to usher them in. Nell had a brief impression of a spacious, white-walled hall and then she was in the drawing-room, which ran the whole width of the house from front to back. A beautiful bright room, with furniture a tasteful blend of old and new.

A lot of people had already arrived. James Fenton, whom Philip had introduced as his partner, detached himself from a group and came towards Nell. 'Hallo, Miss Ramsay. We met in London, if you remember.' He asked her what she would like to drink, and called to a passing girl, 'Come and meet Colonel Whitehead's granddaughter, Bobbie, then you can get her a drink.'

The girl called Bobbie, a curvy blonde with a good deal of make-up, stopped beside them. She was introduced as James' younger sister, but bore little resemblance to him, in either looks or manner. As if he sensed her thoughts James remarked that there were fifteen years between them. 'Sometimes I feel old enough to be her father!'

He stayed beside her, a quiet serious man with courteous manners and an unexpected, dry sense of humour. Nell liked him and they were still talking when Philip, circulating among his guests, stopped for a word. 'Glad you decided to come, Nell. Elizabeth said you might be spending the weekend in London.'

He smiled down at her, and she felt, as so often before in his company, that odd little jolt of discomposure. Other men didn't affect her like this, she thought crossly. She had been getting on splendidly with James Fenton until their host arrived.

Mrs Middleton-Massey approached them, gin and tonic clasped in a large hand. 'Nell, m'dear! Spoken to the girls yet? They're over there with Andrew MacFarlane.'

Nell was about to move in their direction when the older woman clamped a firm hand round her arm. 'Things going all right at home? No repercussions now you're working again?'

She shook her head, very conscious of Philip's eyes on her, and wishing Mrs Middleton-Massey wouldn't ask such personal questions in public.

'As I've told you, my dear man, this girl's had a hard time of it. All the more to her credit that she made the grade, don't you think?'

'Oh, undoubtedly,' Philip agreed smoothly, and studied Nell over the rim of his glass. As if he sensed her embarrassment, James asked her to introduce him to Andrew MacFarlane. Gratefully she moved away with him and under his breath he said, 'That woman handles horses better than humans!'

Nell was delighted to see her old friends again. Pamela Middleton-Massey, who was nearest to her in age, and the the only unmarried one, took her into a corner behind the grand piano. 'I don't care if it's anti-social, but it's been such ages, Nell.' They talked for a long time, catching up on each other's affairs, then Pamela leant towards Nell. 'Things have changed around here, haven't they? What do you think of the master of the house?' She asked this half jokingly, but her eyes were intent.

Nell shrugged. 'All right if you like the type.'

'Does that mean you don't?'

'I prefer Mr Fenton.'

'You've got to be joking!' Pamela's eyes opened very wide. An outdoor girl with a good complexion and a sturdy build, in thirty years she would resemble her mother. She was like her already in her outspokenness. 'I could really go for that man,' she said dreamily. 'All that lovely money, and good-looking too! What more can a girl ask?'

Uneasily Nell glanced over her shoulders, but no one was near enough to hear.

'It's all right,' Pamela said cheerfully. 'And I know it's no use. There's too much competition. That's part of it over there.' She jerked her head to the group around Philip. He was smiling down at the small blonde girl by his side, James' sister. As they watched, Bobbie slipped a hand through his arm and made some remark that had everyone laughing.

'Unfair, isn't it?' Pamela said wistfully. 'Those little blonde women have it made. And she's his partner's sister, so she's bound to see a lot of him.'

'Do they live near here?' asked Nell.

'In London, I think, but they often come to stay. She rides like a sack of potatoes!' Pamela had her mother's good seat on a horse.

When the last of the visitors had gone they went in to lunch. There were a dozen of them around the big table, an aunt of Philip's, his sister and her family, the Fentons, Nell and her relatives. She sat between James Fenton and Philip's brother-in-law, who spent most of the meal keeping his obstreperous youngsters under control. That left Nell to talk to James, which she thoroughly enjoyed doing. She was in the middle of an animated discussion on modern music when she caught Philip's eye on her. His expression was thoughtful, and when she returned his look with a touch of defiance, he registered open amusement.

James was saying something about Bartok, whom Nell detested. She said so, to find that Philip had heard her remark, due to a sudden lull in the conversation.

'That makes two of us, Nell. Debussy is modern enough for me.'

Then the conversation opened up again and James remarked casually that she should hear Philip's piano playing. He was good enough to have made a career of it. Nell was intrigued. She glanced at Philip again, studying the strong features and square jaw, the wide shoulders and large but well shaped hands.

'You surprise me,' she admitted. 'I thought he was an outdoor man in his spare time.'

'He is,' James agreed, 'but he has wide interests. Did you notice the paintings in the drawing-room?'

She had, and for that matter there were a couple of modern landscapes on the wall in front of her. Nell knew enough about art to recognise their worth.

'You mean he regards them as an investment?' Now what on earth had made her say that? It sounded petty, especially when she was in the man's house.

James gave her a straight look. 'You don't know much about Philip if you think that,' he said quietly, and Nell had the grace to blush.

'Well, I don't, Mr Fenton. I haven't really seen a great deal of him, for all that he visits my grandfather so often. I only meant that—that business men do buy paintings with an eye to their market value.'

'Possibly. But Philip isn't really a business man.'

She gazed at him in bewilderment. 'But surely he owns Trent Electronics? The two of you, at least,' she added hastily, thinking that this was her day for unfortunate re-marks.

James shook his head. 'Of course he owns it, but the business side is my concern. Philip can't be bothered with it.'

This was even more surprising. 'You mean he's a ... a sleeping partner, don't they call it?' So that explained why he seemed to have so much free time.

James gave his quiet laugh. 'I must tell Philip that! My dear girl, if it wasn't for him there would be no Trent Electronics! He supplies the capital *and* the brains.' Seeing that she was still at a loss he enlarged. The two of them had met at Cambridge, where James was reading Economics and Philip Mathematics. 'Then he stayed on to do Physics. He has a double First, Miss Ramsay. He was a very brilliant student. The outstanding man in his year.'

'I see,' Nell managed. 'So—so do you mean that he's the firm's chief designer?'

'Right, my dear girl.' James' rather solemn face broke into his rare smile. 'A very talented and creative one. Which is why we're doing so well in the export market.' He went on to tell her that Philip had inherited wealth, so that they had had the initial capital to start the firm, and then Philip's brother-in-law, temporarily relieved of his children by their great-aunt's attention, turned towards her.

While she made polite conversation with him on the surface, Nell was mulling over James' words. She had been so firmly entrenched in her conviction that Philip was a typical go-getting business man that she found it difficult to adjust to the reality. When she had the opportunity she leant towards James and murmured, 'Don't tell Philip what I thought.'

He regarded her gravely. 'Why not, Miss Ramsay?'

'Because he might be offended. After all, it's not very flattering to be thought a—a rich dilettante.'

'All right,' James agreed. 'I won't tell him, though I doubt if he'd be offended. Philip can take a joke against himself.'

Unassailable because of absolute self-confidence, thought Nell. They had reached the liqueur stage, but she decided she had had enough. She didn't want to make any more naïve remarks, and alcohol had a bad habit of loosening her tongue.

'You and James seem to hit it off rather well,' commented Philip, stopping beside her as she stood in the hall to admire one of his pictures.

They had just left the dining-room and most people had moved back into the drawing-room. 'I like him,' Nell answered. 'He was telling me how he first got to know you. I had no idea you were a scientist.'

'Hardly that,' he said casually. 'An applied scientist, I suppose, if I must have a label.'

Bobbie Fenton came down the wide curving staircase, make-up fresh, hair newly combed. She seemed the sort of girl who was over-conscious of her appearance and its impact on men. Nell found her tiresome, with her kittenish manner and her exaggerated femininity, but Philip seemed genuinely fond of her. They moved into the drawing-room, the tall man between the two girls. Philip crossed to Colonel Whitehead's side, concerned lest the old man might be overtiring himself.

'There's a sofa next door, if you feel like a nap, sir.'

While her grandfather protested that he had never felt better, Bobbie had a few words with Nell. 'You're not quite what I expected,' she remarked, an odd trace of petulance on her pretty face.

Nell was amused. 'What did you expect, Miss Fenton?'

'Oh ... I don't know ... more of a Women's Libber ... a dedicated career woman.'

'I am a dedicated career woman,' Nell smiled, then amended that to, 'At least I care about my career. I mean I care about my work.'

'Do you really?' Bobbie asked guilelessly. 'I'm only working until I can find some lovely man to support me.' She accompanied these words with a wistful look in Philip's direction. Though Nell rather despised fluffy, silly little girls, she couldn't help feeling sorry for Bobbie. If she was in love with Philip she was almost certainly in for heartbreak. Brilliant successful men were apt to demand more than just a pretty face.

Elizabeth's mind seemed to work on the same lines. When they were back in their own house, having mugs of hot chocolate before they retired to bed, she asked Nell how she had enjoyed herself.

'It was great, Elizabeth. I didn't expect to have such a good time.'

In fact she had spent most of the afternoon entertaining

Philip's nephews and nieces, thereby incurring the grati-
tude of their hard-pressed parents.

'I'm surprised you enjoyed it. I thought you'd be bored
to tears helping with those awful brats.'

'Not awful, just high-spirited.' Nell had always got on
well with children, even when they were ill and frightened.
The paediatric specialist had once been heard to comment
that he would be delighted to have Miss Ramsay as his
house physician.

Elizabeth yawned delicately. 'Well, anyway, it was good
of you to help out. That silly little sister of James' might
have had the decency to do the same, instead of fawning
over Philip in that sickening way.'

Nell studied her aunt curiously. Elizabeth's expression
was disagreeable. It made her look older and less attractive.
'Not that she has a hope,' the other woman added, speaking more to herself than to her niece. 'Can you see a man
like Philip falling for a brainless little idiot like that?'

'Not really. I imagine—when—if he marries, it will be
someone very different.'

'Exactly,' Elizabeth agreed, good humour restored.
'Someone mature and intelligent.' She put down her mug,
rose and gazed into the mirror that hung just behind her.
What she saw appeared to please her, and indeed she looked
very attractive tonight, in an amber-coloured dress softly
gathered at yoke and waist. In the subdued light of the
standard lamp she could have passed as no older than
Philip. Was she really thinking of herself when she made
that last remark? It looked like it, and for all Nell knew
Philip had given Elizabeth good reason to think it.

He had certainly been very attentive today, not only to
Colonel Whitehead, but to the Colonel's daughter. Elizabeth would make an admirable wife for a man who enter-
tained on the scale that Philip did. She was poised, elegant,
well bred, and she was undoubtedly very fond of him. In
love? Nell didn't know, couldn't imagine her cool reserved

aunt losing her head over any man. Would Philip be content with such a relationship? He looked a man of strong feeling. He had undeniable physical attraction.

'Well, I'm for bed,' Elizabeth decided. 'I'll look in to see Father on my way. You needn't bother.'

Although they were on more friendly terms than they had been, there was still the odd moment when Elizabeth needed to stress the fact that she was the one who was closest to the old man. Nell smiled wryly to herself, gathered up the mugs and took them into the kitchen to rinse. She stood at the sink, the tap running, and into her mind flashed a picture of Philip as he had looked this afternoon, when he had stood beside her in the hall.

He had smiled down at her from his considerable height and she, well wined and dined, had felt none of the wariness she usually experienced in his company. In fact she had been momentarily attracted by that blend of toughness and intelligence, a fact which she was reluctant to admit now. And what was she doing, thinking about the wretched man at this hour of the night? she asked herself crossly, then rinsed the mugs out, dried them briskly and took herself off to bed.

On Easter Monday they were staying at home and entertaining some elderly relatives, who lived in the same county. Nell wasn't looking forward to their visit with much enthusiasm, having already seen them on a previous weekend and been submitted to a heavy-handed catechism of her affairs, which had ended in laboriously expressed disapproval. Great-Uncle Lionel and his wife Marina, with their two spinster daughters, older than Elizabeth and set in their ways! Not an inspiring foursome, thought Nell, as their stately old Bentley, driven by the younger of her two aunts, drew up by the front door.

Even Elizabeth had had some doubts and had asked Nell if she would care to invite some young company round.

But Pamela Middleton-Massey was engaged and she didn't care to inflict her dreary relatives on anyone else. Perhaps there was a good film on television, and if she put herself out to please throughout lunch, they wouldn't think her rude if she disappeared afterwards. They had pheasant, shot on the estate and perfectly cooked by Elizabeth, who was an excellent housewife when she had to be. Nell drank more wine than usual to fortify herself against the relatives, and earned a black mark from Marina as a result. They were lingering over coffee when the telephone rang.

'Would you answer it, Nell?' asked Elizabeth.

A cheerful young voice rang in her ear. 'Can I speak to Nell, please?'

She recognised him at once. 'That's Johnny, isn't it?' Johnny Monckton, who was the elder of Philip's two nephews, and whom she had met yesterday.

'Yes, it is. We were wondering, Nell, if you could bear to come round and play with us? Mum and Dad have gone out and so has Uncle Philip. I wish you would, Nell. We're so *bored*! There's only a soppy old musical on telly and the little ones keep quarrelling when we play games.'

'But surely your parents haven't left you on your own?' Nell, who had done her stint as a student in the accident department, was horrified at the thought.

' 'Course not. The Prices are here, but they're so boring.'

The Prices were the husband and wife who ran Philip's home so competently. Nell felt sorry for the children. It was rather mean of the adults to leave them to their own devices.

'All right, Johnny, I'll come over for an hour or two. When do you think your parents and your uncle will be back?'

'Dunno! Gosh Nell, that's super. Come right away.'

CHAPTER SIX

THE hour or two stretched through into the evening. Nell found the children sprawled on the floor in the small sitting-room, in front of a log fire. Television blared unheeded in the corner, while Johnny and his younger brother argued over a game of cards. Their sister Jackie had retreated behind the sofa and was reading a battered old annual without much enthusiasm.

Five minutes later they were happily engaged in an uproarious game of Beggar my Neighbour, and when Philip opened the door on them they were so engrossed that they didn't hear him. Nell was slamming her cards down with as much enthusiasm as the children, and shouting just as loudly, when she caught a movement out of the corner of her eye. She looked up, was surprised to see Philip returned so soon, and jumped quickly to her feet.

His expression was a blend of curiosity and amusement. 'This is an unexpected pleasure, my dear Nell. To what do we owe the honour?'

At once she felt a fool, an intruder, and only too conscious of her hot and untidy appearance. 'The children were bored,' she mumbled. 'They asked me to come over. But now that you're back——'

Philip laid a firm hand on her shoulder. 'Please don't run away. You can't leave in the middle of a game.' He sat down and picked up a newspaper. 'Don't mind me, kids! If you can bear the noise, so can I!'

So they finished the game, which ended in a victory for Johnny, though Nell, selfconscious now in Philip's presence, behaved with less abandon. She rose and turned a little awkwardly to him.

'I didn't mean to intrude, but I thought you were all going to be out for some time. If I'd realised——'

He stood as well. 'My dear girl, what are you apologising for? It was very kind of you to come, though they shouldn't have bothered you. If they'd listened to what I told them they'd have known I was only going out for half an hour.'

He had been driving some of his visitors to the station, apparently. Everyone had left now, except for his sister's family. 'And your father and mother need the occasional break if they're to stay sane,' Philip ended with a ferocious glare at the three children.

They threw themselves on him, giggling and demanding, 'Uncle Philip, can Nell stay for tea?'

'Can she, Uncle Philip?'

'She'll stay if you ask her.'

'I'm not too sure of that,' joked Philip, one corner of his mouth quirking as he looked across the children's heads at Nell.

She bit her lip, unsure if he really wanted her. Children were so tactless! He could hardly tell her to go away. 'I think I'd better get home,' she said hesitantly, and at that everyone, Philip included, looked disappointed.

They asked her if she had anything special to do. Remembering the dreary relatives, Nell laughed and said no.

'Then stay,' Philip urged. 'It'll make their day.'

So she stayed and they had another game of Beggar my Neighbour, ate an enormous and delicious tea, played Snakes and Ladders and Sorry, and finally gathered round the fire to watch Philip perform conjuring tricks.

'You're very good!' Nell exclaimed admiringly as he palmed coins dexterously and drew table tennis balls from the children's ears.

'I think so too,' he agreed with cheerful lack of modesty. 'Should be after all the practice I've put in!'

The telephone rang and he answered it. 'Oh, hallo,

Elizabeth! Yes, she is still here. Do you want to speak to her? I see … I'll pass it on. Goodbye, my dear.' As he replaced the telephone he told Nell that her relatives were leaving. 'Elizabeth seemed a little put out that you weren't there to say goodbye. I didn't realise you had visitors.'

'I did my duty at lunch,' Nell retorted airily, to receive a thoughtful look.

'Not a great girl for family life, are you?'

Sensing criticism, she went pink. 'I have a lot of very stuffy relatives. Perhaps you're luckier in yours. Oh well, I suppose I'd better go and say goodbye.'

'Elizabeth said there wasn't much point. That they were tired of waiting for you.'

Then why had she bothered to ring? To make Nell feel awkward, more than likely. That was the way her aunt's mind seemed to work. Nell sighed, tried to think of something to say, but was spared the need because the children were clamouring for more conjuring tricks. Watching Philip juggling expertly with billiard balls a few minutes later, she marvelled at the change in the man. Or perhaps if she was honest the change was in herself.

In the children's boisterous company she had forgotten her antagonism, relaxed, let her hair down, had fun. Perhaps she had been too hasty in her judgment, for in her experience anyone who was as good with children as Philip was must be a fundamentally decent person.

When the children's parents returned the youngsters were borne off to bed. 'Much too late,' their mother reprimanded, 'and quite out of hand.' She gave her brother an affectionate look. 'Thanks for the respite, Phil. We needed a break,' and to Nell with genuine warmth, 'It was good of you to help. Give the girl a stiff drink. I'm sure she needs it!'

Philip brushed aside Nell's protests that she really ought to go. 'They know where you are. Stay to supper—you've certainly earned it!'

At ease with him as she had never been before, Nell accepted happily. The Moncktons were pleasant uncomplicated people, so that it was an agreeable foursome, and after supper Philip was persuaded to play the piano. Well fed and relaxed, Nell leant back in her chair, shut her eyes and became totally absorbed in the music.

'James Fenton was right. Your brother is good enough to be a professional,' she said under her breath, when Philip stopped for a smoke.

Alicia nodded with sisterly pride. 'Philip has all the talent in our family,' she remarked with engaging lack of envy. 'Just as well I'm a woman, so I don't have to compete.'

'Are there only the two of you?'

'Yes. We've always been close. I have a super brother, Nell. A pity he hasn't a family of his own.'

'Perhaps he's thinking of getting married, though.' Nell's glance strayed round the room. 'It's such a lovely house, but far too big for a man on his own.'

'Perhaps,' Alicia agreed with a smile. 'Though if he is he's keeping it very close. I think myself he just wanted a place in the country. We grew up on a farm, you know, and he missed the life when he started the London office.'

'I didn't know,' said Nell.

Alicia nodded and went on, 'A place like yours really. An old country house. Father wanted him to stay in Devon and run the estate, but Philip had other ideas. Our grandmother was on his side, and when she died she left him most of her money. So he launched into the electronics business. He'd have been wasted as a full-time farmer.'

'So now he's a part-time one! Does he have a good manager?' Nell asked, thinking of the problems her grandfather had had.

'An excellent one. Haven't you met him yet?' Alicia sounded faintly surprised, so she obviously didn't realise that this evening wasn't a typical one, Nell thought wryly.

She probably assumed that they were good friends, living so close to each other.

This cosy little chat was broken up as the men joined them by the fire. When Nell·looked at the clock a few minutes later she was astounded to find that it was past eleven. Philip insisted on walking her home when she turned down his offer of a lift.

They stepped out briskly through the cold and starry night, not saying much, quiet and relaxed in a companionable sort of way. Nell came to a halt under the old wrought iron lantern that hung above the Manor's great front door. 'It's been nice, Philip,' and feeling that inadequate, 'No, it's been absolutely great. I enjoyed myself tremendously.'

He smiled, put out a finger and ran it lightly down her smooth young cheek. 'I believe you really did. Know something? You've made a great hit with the kids.'

They parted on the best of terms, but Nell's contentment was short-lived. As she tiptoed softly down the corridor to her bedroom Elizabeth spoke through her half open door.

'It *was* tea you were invited to, wasn't it? I hope you didn't outstay your welcome.' The light voice had a peevish ring to it.

Nell pushed the door open, determined not to let herself be rattled. 'They wanted me to stay. Honestly, Aunt Elizabeth.'

'I've told you before, I wish you'd drop the aunt.' She put down her book and beat a tattoo on the pink silk bedspread. 'Philip was probably just being polite. A bit ... gauche of you to think he meant it.'

In just such a way had Elizabeth deflated the child Nell, many years ago. The unkind words no longer had power to hurt, because Nell was an adult now and could meet Elizabeth on equal terms.

'Philip's not the sort of man to make polite gestures,'

Nell said quietly. 'We had a super evening and you're not going to spoil it.'

Elizabeth's laughter was a trifle forced. 'What a touchy little thing you are! I just don't like to see you make a fool of yourself.'

'I don't know why you're so cross about it,' said Nell unwisely. 'You're always telling me to be more agreeable to Philip.'

'Well, naturally I expect you to be courteous to my friends.' Elizabeth put on her long-suffering face. 'I shouldn't have to remind you, though, that Philip is my friend, not yours, Nell.'

This was an astonishing remark from the poised and sophisticated Elizabeth. It had a ring of the nursery about it. Perhaps she had made similar remarks to her sister thirty years ago. Nell started to laugh and Elizabeth gave her a hostile look.

'May I share the joke?'

Nell bit her lip and made a helpless little gesture with one hand. 'I was thinking ...' Caution prevailed and she modified her original sentence, 'We sound like a pair of quarrelling children. He's *my* friend! No, he's mine! Honestly, Elizabeth, this is too silly.'

She would have done better to stay silent. The hostile expression changed to one of outrage. Elizabeth had never had much sense of humour and Nell had offended her dignity.

'Go away,' she managed in a choked voice. 'You're a troublemaker, just like your mother. I suppose I have to put up with you for Father's sake, but you needn't think I enjoy doing it!'

It was the remark about her mother that caused Nell's control to slip. 'I'm only too aware how much you dislike me. Believe me, the feeling's mutual!' and she slammed out of the room, as angry as Elizabeth.

Once she had simmered down she felt very ashamed. Her aunt had been unpleasant, unreasonable, absurdly possessive in her remarks about Philip, but it would have been more adult to ignore her, not to get involved in a childish and distasteful row. Nell spent a restless and unhappy night, and was only able to compose herself for sleep when she decided to make it up with Elizabeth in the morning.

On Tuesday Nell went for an early ride before her aunt was up. She arrived back at the Manor to find Blackie having her mid-mornings in the kitchen.

'Know where Aunt Elizabeth is?' asked Nell.

'On the terrace. What have you done to her, dearie?' Blackie's face crinkled with worry. 'When I mentioned your name she practically spat at me.'

Nell sighed. 'We had a row last night. Pour me a cup of coffee and I'll go and make my peace with her.'

Elizabeth sat on the terrace, stiff-backed and set-faced. If she saw Nell's approach she gave no sign of it. The girl sat down at the opposite end of the stone bench. 'Elizabeth?' No answer. 'Elizabeth!' Nell leant towards the older woman, praying for the right words to soften that stony face. 'I'm ... sorry about last night. Couldn't we ... forget about it?'

'I have always tried to get on with you,' said Elizabeth coldly. 'It's you who has been difficult, Nell.'

So she was not prepared to meet her niece half way. Nell choked back an angry retort, reminding herself that she was doing this for her grandfather—yes, and for Blackie too, because family quarrels were apt to involve the whole household.

'We both lost our tempers,' she said quietly, 'and we said things we didn't mean. Grandpa will be so upset if we're on bad terms. Please, Elizabeth, for his sake let's try to be friends.'

A faint colour tinged Elizabeth's usually pale complexion. Staring straight ahead of her, she spoke in a cool controlled voice. 'All right, Nell. I accept your apology. I only hope it's sincere.' The light eyes turned to survey her niece. The smooth face was quite expressionless. What went on behind that mask? Nell wondered despairingly. There was no warmth in her aunt's manner, no true desire to be friends. Elizabeth saw herself as the wronged one. It had not occurred to her that she was as much at fault as the girl. 'More,' Nell thought crossly. 'But I'm the one who does the apologising!' She downed her coffee quickly, muttered something and walked away.

At least the little scene had cleared the air, but it had left her tense and irritable. Nell sighed, then took a deep breath. It was such a beautiful day, bright, breezy, made for enjoyment, not for the pettiness of family bickering. She called the dogs, who were circling on the lower lawn, and took them off for a walk, through the woods that stretched for miles along this side of the river.

In spite of Elizabeth's ungenerous response Nell was glad she had made that move towards reconciliation. At least they could meet at meals without awkwardness, maintain a civilised façade in front of visitors, play cards in the evening with her grandfather. Philip would drop in sometimes for a round of bridge, partnering Elizabeth while Nell played with the old man.

'Not much good, are you, miss?' he growled one evening, when they had suffered their usual defeat at the hands of the other pair.

Nell laughed as she threw her cards down. 'I know, Grandpa. I find it so difficult to remember the tricks.'

Elizabeth looked contemptuous, Philip amused. 'Tell you what, little one,' he said carelessly, 'I'll give you a chance to beat me at something else. You did say you played chess?'

They sat facing each other over a low table, and though she was determined to give him a good game, Nell found it difficult to concentrate. She was distracted by that long brown hand moving the pieces with such decision, while her own hovered uncertainly over the white men. When he wasn't making a move he sat with his chin in his hands, staring down at the board with total concentration. Nell envied him this ability to divorce himself so absolutely from his surroundings, all too conscious of the sharp glances coming their way from the card table, where Elizabeth was playing bezique with her father.

When their game ended the Colonel announced his intention of retiring. Elizabeth usually went to bed by eleven, but this evening she sat on by the fire, an open book on her knee. Philip made a move, glanced at his watch and gave an exclamation.

'That late? Pity to stop now, when we've reached the end game.'

Nell gave her aunt an uncertain glance, which Philip intercepted. 'Don't feel you have to stay up, Elizabeth,' he said pleasantly. 'Nell can lock up after me.'

'I'm in no hurry.' Elizabeth's answer was quick and a shade irritable. 'This book is quite riveting,' which considering that she hadn't turned a page for some minutes, Nell thought less than the truth.

Philip took her remark at its face value, nodded and became once more absorbed in planning his next move. Nell fought a losing battle, but hung on longer than she had expected. As twelve struck Elizabeth sighed audibly and closed her book with a snap.

'I should have expected you to beat Nell far more quickly,' she commented as she crossed the room to stand behind his chair.

His smile was rueful. 'So should I. I didn't realise she was this good.'

'Lucky fluke,' said Nell lightly, wishing her aunt wouldn't subject her to that unnerving stare.

'I think I'll go to bed,' Elizabeth announced. 'I have a busy day tomorrow.'

'Mm? Goodnight, Elizabeth,' Philip murmured abtractedly, giving her only half his attention. Usually a man of punctilious manners, he didn't rise from his chair as she left the room, and a flicker of annoyance crossed Elizabeth's face.

After her aunt had gone Nell's defences collapsed quickly and Philip gave her check less than ten minutes later. 'Check and mate,' he amended, making his last move. As he piled the chessmen back into the beautifully carved box that belonged to her grandfather, he smiled at her across the table. The standard lamp behind his chair held them in a circle of light, while the rest of the room was in semi-darkness. It created a feeling of intimacy, so that she stirred uneasily and looked away from his bright intelligent eyes.

'Golly, I'm tired!' She rubbed her eyes and stiffened when his fingers closed round her wrist. He pulled her hands away firmly.

'Bad for them, doctor! You ought to know that.'

His face was very near to hers. He rested one hand on the table so that he came even closer. Nell's heart started to thump in her chest, and her breathing quickened. Philip's smile was teasing, as if he knew exactly the effect he was having on her.

'You don't look in the least tired,' he observed. 'In fact you look extremely pretty and very ... desirable.' The last word came out almost with tenderness.

Nell blinked and tried hard for a nonchalant approach. 'Are you trying to make a pass at me, Philip?' She half rose from her chair, but the little table was too close to her knees, and she had to drop back again.

Philip picked it up unceremoniously and dumped it to one side. 'Not trying, Nell,' he announced, 'making one,' and he drew her to her feet and into his arms. His kisses were expert and very satisfying. His hands on her body evoked sensations Nell had never experienced before. She wanted to abandon herself entirely to physical delight, but when a door banged in the quiet house sanity returned. If Elizabeth came back on some excuse and found them like this ... She tore herself out of Philip's arms, ran shaking hands over her tumbled hair, and retreated to the fireplace.

'It's time we went to bed,' she stammered, saw by his smile that she had chosen the words unfortunately, and endeavoured to retrieve them.

'You know quite well what I meant! It's time to say goodnight.'

He took his dismissal easily and a small corner of Nell's mind was piqued that he should. She tried to think of a cutting remark as she accompanied him across the hall, but her thoughts were scattered and incoherent. He turned the heavy key in the lock and opened the outer door on to a wet and windy night.

'Simmer down, young Nell,' he advised, and ruffled her hair lightly. 'You're a big girl now. Surely you can take a few kisses in your stride?' He laughed and was gone, closing the heavy door between them.

The key turned stiffly. The bolt stuck for a moment. Nell gave it a savage push to relieve her feelings, and climbed the stairs slowly. Damn Philip and his expertise at love-making! He had felt in the mood and she had been available—that was all it had meant to him, and she had been a fool to get so carried away. She lacked his casual sophistication. She was not as experienced as he was.

When she reached the top of the stairs a door opened. Elizabeth, in a blue quilted wrap, emerged from the bathroom, eyes narrowing as they took in her niece's flushed and dishevelled appearance.

'So I was right!' she gritted, hands clenching and unclenching at her side. 'You were determined to get Philip on his own.' There was a note of near-hysteria in her voice.

'You scheming little bitch, you're just like your mother—
after every man in sight, totally promiscuous!'

Nell shook her head wearily, too confused to retaliate.
'Please, Elizabeth, don't make a scene. So all right, Philip
kissed me. It didn't mean a thing. He made that quite
obvious.'

Perhaps there was an unconscious wistfulness in her
voice, for Elizabeth smiled suddenly and maliciously. 'Of
course it didn't mean a thing. Philip's a normal man. He'll
take what's offered, and you make it so obvious, my dear
Nell.' Her hands stilled at last and she swept into her room.

This time, Nell thought, this time her aunt must be the one
to apologise. Elizabeth had gone too far, made insulting
remarks that would be difficult to forgive or forget. She
rose before seven, made herself a hasty breakfast, left a
note on the kitchen table for Blackie, and drove off to the
Middleton-Masseys' house to borrow one of their horses.

On a windswept plateau, with not a house in sight and
only the distant sound of a tractor to make her feel less
alone, she came to terms with her problem. Either she had
to leave Lanmore or she had to find some way to overcome
Elizabeth's hostility. There had been something unpleas-
antly close to hatred in her aunt's eyes during those moments on the bedroom landing. How much of that emotion
was due to her dislike of Nell's mother and how much to
her infatuation with Philip? If it was mainly jealousy then
Nell's course was plain. Steer clear of Philip. Give her aunt
no cause to consider her a rival. But if the problem lay far
deeper, lost in the traumas of early childhood, if she was
hated because she was her mother's daughter, then, thought
Nell unhappily, there really was no solution.

Her grandfather might know, but she couldn't possibly
worry the old man. Blackie could almost certainly supply
an answer, but she was too partisan to be objective. Dr
MacFarlane? He had known them all since before Nell was

born. She would go and see him, ask his advice and hope
that he could help her.

She telephoned Dr MacFarlane from the village pub
where she had lunch, and returned to Lanmore at three
o'clock. The doctor was in his house, waiting for her. A
man of few words, he wasted no time on the social niceties
but ushered her into his small room where he saw private
patients.

'Well, my dear, what is it?' A rueful glance at the clock.
'I have a couple of visits to make, so I'd appreciate it if
you'd get to the point.'

Thus urged, Nell did her best. She stammered a little to
begin with, while Dr MacFarlane sat at the big desk, head
down and brows drawn together in a frown of concentration. He was a good listener and Nell got it all out, trying
hard for objectivity, simply stating facts. She ended up with
an appeal for help.

'You've known us all so long, Dr Mac. You've been a
good friend, and I do need help.'

'So does Elizabeth,' Dr Mac answered dryly, looking up
at last to give one of his penetrating stares. Under that uncomfortably direct glance Nell's cheeks began to burn.

'So you think it's all my fault,' she said defeatedly.
'You're on Elizabeth's side?'

'Child! Child!' The doctor's tone was gently admonish-
ing. 'I'm on nobody's side, but her problems are greater
than yours. She's at a difficult stage in a woman's life, when
she sees her youth slipping away, her hopes of marriage
nearly gone. Of course she resents you. You're young and
pretty, with your whole life ahead of you.'

'And the other things I told you? About my mother?
And . . . about Philip?'

'I am not God,' Dr MacFarlane pronounced, heavily
sarcastic. 'I cannot read people's minds.' He followed these
portentous remarks with an unexpected twinkling smile.
'Oh, Nell, Nell, you should have studied enough psycholgy

to know that motives are usually mixed. It doesn't help that
your aunt and your mother never got on. It doesn't help
that she is—or fancies she is—in love with Trent.' He
looked down at his blotter, his mouth compressed. 'I'll talk
to Elizabeth. I'll call after I've made my visits. Now be a
good girl and go away.'

Nell went off not too unhappily. Deciding to stay away
until after Dr MacFarlane's visit, she rode back to the
Middleton-Masseys' and spent the rest of the afternoon
with them. By the time she returned home the doctor had
been and gone—that much was obvious from Elizabeth's
opening remark.

'So you've been telling tales to Sandy,' her aunt said
softly, putting down the vase of daffodils she was carrying
and straightening to look at her niece.

Nell's heart was thumping with apprehension. Not
another scene! she thought. Surely, surely Dr Mac had
persuaded her aunt to be reasonable? 'I went to him for
advice,' she answered quietly. 'I think you'll agree that we
do need some help.'

'Speak for yourself, Nell!' The older woman's voice was
acid. 'However, Sandy is right. Father mustn't be upset.
We owe it to him that his last years should be happy ones.'
Elizabeth was given to saying things like that, which always had the effect of making Nell horribly embarrassed.
Difficult to answer too, and Elizabeth was waiting for a
reply.

'Of course,' Nell mumbled, ill at ease and inarticulate.
'Yes, of course, Elizabeth.'

'So we have to make an effort, Nell. Keep the peace for
Father's sake. I shall certainly do my best.' She tilted her
head and looked down her long nose at the girl, a habit that
Nell had always found disconcerting.

'Oh, so will I,' she agreed hastily, and put out a tentative
hand towards her aunt.

Elizabeth chose to ignore this. She gave a brisk nod,

drew a finger across the old oak dresser behind her, frowned at the trace of dust on it, and departed in the direction of the kitchen. So with this exchange Nell had to be content. It was a truce, which was at least better than open warfare. On the surface life would go on as before, though she was sure she would always feel ill at ease in her aunt's company.

One thing she was quite determined about. She would stay away from Philip, not only to avoid rows with her aunt, but for her own peace of mind. She didn't want to remember the effect he had on her. She would take good care not to be alone with him again.

She was relieved to learn that he had gone off to Copenhagen and Stockholm—some business trip—a meeting with potential customers, her grandfather said. 'Brainy chap, Philip,' he commented. 'He's tried to explain his work to me, but I'm a fool over physics. You'd probably understand, Nell.'

They were having tea alone, just the two of them, for Elizabeth was at a W.I. meeting. Nell laughed and told her grandfather that she doubted it. A-levels were as far as she could have gone in pure science. 'When I think about it now I'm staggered that I ever passed physics. But I was dead keen to do medicine, so I suppose that spurred me on.'

Her grandfather harrumphed, a trick he had when he was about to come out with something important. 'Sandy says you're a good doctor. That I ought to be proud of you.'

He was staring into the fire and Nell gave him a loving look. 'And aren't you?' she teased.

'Harrumph!' the Colonel went again, turned a dull red and scowled at his granddaughter. 'You needn't think I approve of your career—or ever will—but since you've taken it on the least you can do is be good at it.'

And that was as near as he ever came to admitting that Dr MacFarlane was right.

CHAPTER SEVEN

A FORTNIGHT passed before Nell remembered that she hadn't talked to her family about Blackie, then one morning she went into the kitchen to find the housekeeper slumped at the table, looking very flushed.

'I get these turns now and then, Nell. Don't fuss, dear. I'll be all right.'

Blackie was nearly as bad as Nell's grandfather in her abhorrence of all things medical. Reluctantly she allowed Nell to feel her pulse, and admitted that she had been suffering from increasing bouts of giddiness for quite a long time.

'And headaches?'

'Everyone has headaches now and then,' Blackie said evasively, and Nell laughed in spite of her unease.

'Thank goodness you're not really my patient! When did you last see Dr Mac?'

'Not for years. There's nothing wrong with me,' Blackie said stoutly, her colour beginning to return to normal. 'Is there?' she added, apprehension showing through her defiance.

'Oh, Blackie!' Nell gave the older woman a hug. 'Maybe you've been overdoing it. I'm ashamed that I forgot to talk to Grandpa about the house.'

'You've had problems of your own,' said Blackie, returning the hug affectionately. 'Pity people can't be renovated like houses, dearie!'

'They can sometimes,' Nell smiled. 'Made to work more effieciently anyway! We all need help as we get older. Go and see Dr Mac, and I'll talk to Grandpa and Aunt Elizabeth about the house.'

That evening she told them bluntly that if they didn't do something about lightening Blackie's work load they might lose her.

'Millie comes in three mornings from the village,' Elizabeth protested, but Nell shook her head.

'It's not enough. This house is so old-fashioned. The kitchen needs major renovations. The bathrooms too, and the floors.'

'Solid oak planks. Nothing wrong with them,' the Colonel said indignantly.

'They need sanding and polishing and sealing. Oh, Grandpa, you must spend some money on the house! If Blackie has to give up we won't find anyone else willing to take on her job.'

'Blackie give up?' Elizabeth looked horrified.

'I think—mind, I'm not absolutely sure—that she has high blood pressure. She's seeing Dr Mac tomorrow. If she has got it he'll either tell her to rest more, or he'll advise her to give up altogether.'

'I'll think about it,' Colonel Whitehead said tetchily. 'But builder chaps all over the place! Drive me crazy! Cost such a lot!'

'Rubbish!' said Nell firmly. 'Of course you can afford it. You must have made a small fortune on the farm and the land you sold to Philip.'

The Colonel muttered about capital gains tax and the high cost of living, but agreed that financially it could be done. 'Though mind, there'll be less for you girls when I go.'

'I wish you wouldn't talk like that, Father.' When the old man had left the room Elizabeth said thoughtfully, 'If he does agree to modernise the house it would go for far more when we sell it.' At Nell's startled look she added sharply, 'I'm not anticipating Father's death, so don't look so shocked. But I've been thinking for years that we ought to leave this place, find a nice modern house. Something easy to run, like Philip's house.'

'Grandpa would hate it. Can't we stick it out here for as long as possible?'

'We?' Elizabeth asked acidly.

'You, then. But if I decide to join the MacFarlanes' practice I'll be able to help out.'

'As a full-time G.P.? I doubt that. And perhaps Blackie isn't as bad as you think she is.'

But Blackie was worse. Dr MacFarlane spoke to Nell at the end of morning surgery. 'She has severe hypertension. I'm starting her on treatment straight away. You'll have to find temporary help until we see how she does.'

Blackie refused to be an invalid at the Manor, saying it would only make extra work for them. She chose to go and stay with a widowed sister in the district, promising she would be back as soon as Dr MacFarlane gave the word. Colonel Whitehead raised no more objections to Nell's suggestions and the builders were available earlier than expected.

'Say they can start next week,' the old man announced gloomily. 'Not much work hereabouts, so they're delighted to have a big job on hand.'

'And it will be a big job,' Philip remarked, when they told him the news. 'Be much better if you all cleared out and left them to it!' They could stay in his house, he suggested. He had plenty of room and an excellent housekeeper.

The Colonel demurred, but Elizabeth looked pleased. Nell suggested that her grandfather and her aunt should go, and she would find somewhere else. 'The MacFarlanes, perhaps? It would be so handy for work.'

'That might be best,' Elizabeth agreed, but Philip overruled her. One more visitor would make no difference. They might as well stay together, and if his housekeeper couldn't cope she could have extra help. So it was settled and they would be moving in on Monday week. Nell felt a faint unease at the prospect of living in Philip's house, but could think of no good reason for refusing without causing offence.

'I think my aunt would have preferred me to go somewhere else,' she told Andrew after the Thursday surgery. 'She didn't look too pleased when Philip insisted.'

'Then come to us. You'd be most welcome.'

'I know, Andy, and I nearly asked you to have me, but it would be awkward rejecting Philip's offer.' She sighed. 'Life's getting me down. I could do with another break.'

'Then how about coming to London with me this Saturday? Q.C.H. is playing a good team from South Wales.'

Nell was only a moderate enthusiast for rugby, but it would be an opportunity to meet her friends. 'I'd like that, but what about the Saturday morning surgery?'

'We'll leave after the surgery. I'll ask Miss Winter to keep the list small, and we'll take a packed lunch.'

Nell laughed and shook her head. 'Even the way you belt along, we wouldn't make it.'

'We'll be on time for the start,' Andrew promised, and he was right. They made it with ten minutes to spare. Warmly clad in duffle coat and fur-lined boots, Nell wandered away from Andrew, whose whole attention was on the game. She found Jimmy Green with Belinda hanging lovingly on his arm, and joined them for an exchange of gossip.

At half time she introduced them to Andrew, who was less cheerful than usual because the Q.C.H. team was doing badly.

'Thirteen nil down,' he gloomed, 'and they seem to have given up. They're not trying.'

'Is he always like that?' Belinda asked as Andrew's stocky figure plunged through the crowd when the game began again.

'I don't know,' Nell smiled. 'It's the first time we've been to a rugger match together.'

'Make it the last time,' Belinda advised. 'A man who's more interested in a game than the girl he's with isn't worth cultivating.'

Nell laughed and shook her head. 'You've a one-track mind, Belle. I'm not interested in Andrew, so I don't mind what he does.'

'Just as well,' retorted Belinda, 'or poor Ted would be upset.'

At the end of the game Jimmy suggested that they team up and make a night of it.

Nell looked down at herself doubtfully. 'I didn't dress for an evening out.'

'No problem,' Belinda observed. 'Come back to Q.C.H. and I'll lend you something. We've swapped clothes before.'

So clad in a long red dress of Belinda's, with Belinda's make-up on her face and another friend's sandals on her feet, Nell went on the town and thoroughly enjoyed herself. After the strain of recent family life she felt an unaccustomed urge to break out. She drank more than usual, laughed a great deal and didn't worry too much about Andrew's increasing amorousness.

'Thought you said you weren't interested in Andrew,' Belinda remarked, when the two girls were alone in the powder room of the club.

Nell coloured a little. 'I'm not.'

'You could have fooled me,' said Belinda, with an unusual touch of dryness.

'Oh, Belle! Life's been a bit difficult lately,' Nell sighed. 'And Andy's good fun. Besides, Ted's just another friend —I've told you that before.'

'You have an odd way of treating your friends,' Belinda commented disapprovingly. 'Why won't you let him pay you a visit?'

Ted had twice suggested coming down to Lanmore, and both times Nell had put him off. 'Because I don't want him getting too serious. If I let him come down he'll get the wrong idea.'

'It's your life,' Belinda shrugged, leaning close to the mirror to inspect her eye make-up. 'But you've certainly changed. You used to be such a quiet girl.'

And still was beneath the gay exterior. Not even to herself was Nell prepared to admit that she was using Andrew as an antidote to Philip. The thought had risen in her mind, to be quickly suppressed. Why should she need an antidote? She was surely in danger of reading too much into those few kisses they had exchanged. 'But I wish it was Philip here instead of Andrew,' she thought, and felt ashamed of her lack of gratitude. Andrew was doing his best to give her an enjoyable evening. Besides, Philip was too mature to fit into the present company. Jimmy and Belinda might be qualified doctors, but they retained much of their medical student humour. They were not educated outside their own field.

'Hey, Nell!' Jimmy snapped his fingers under her nose. 'We were saying it's time to break this up.'

Nell looked at her watch and pulled a face. 'We won't be back till dawn, Andy, though I suppose it doesn't matter. Tomorrow *is* Sunday.'

'And since it's Sunday we needn't return at all,' Andrew retorted. 'I'm sure we'll find somewhere for the night.'

A hotel? With Andrew? Nell knew what that would mean—an unpleasant scene when he came knocking on her door. It would be her own fault too, for encouraging him all night. Belinda was watching her with a half smile that said quite plainly, 'Serve you right for leading him on!'

'I think we'd better go home,' Nell decided, and Jimmy gave her a horrified look.

'You must be crazy! With all that booze inside him? Want to die young, Nell?'

Nell remembered the way Andrew had belted up the motorway that afternoon and shuddered at the thought. 'I suppose we'd better stay ...' Her words tailed off at the sudden gleam in Andrew's eye.

It was then that Belinda took pity on her. 'You'll never get into a hotel at this hour,' she said firmly. 'We'll find you somewhere in the residents' quarters.' Dear, helpful, bossy Belinda! She overruled Andrew's objections, took them back to College Street, bade a loving farewell to Jimmy and ushered them into the common-room, where a few sleepy residents had still not gone to bed.

Andrew looked at them dourly, plainly disgusted at this end to the evening. 'Get going, boys and girls,' Belinda said briskly. 'This chap wants to doss down on the sofa for the night.'

'Is that so?' enquired a cheeky young doctor. 'And just who is the gentleman, to make so free with hospital property?'

'Dr Andrew MacFarlane,' Belinda announced with a flourish. 'He was a resident here when you were dissecting your first cadaver, so a bit more respect, if you don't mind.'

This raised a laugh, though Andrew didn't smile. He surveyed the sofa nearest to the stove gloomily, while Belinda thumped him cheerfully on the back. 'With a couple of blankets you'll be very snug.'

By the time she returned with them the last of the residents were trailing from the room. Nell was glad to see her friend, because she was afraid that Andrew was about to make a scene. Belinda punched up the cushions, spread out the blankets and patted the sofa invitingly.

'Sleep well. No one will disturb you now.'

'Big deal,' Andrew said glumly. 'Why can't Nell have one of the other sofas?'

Belinda gave him a look of mock horror. 'Because the R.S.O. wouldn't approve, that's why. And the dear man's often up at night.'

'You said I wouldn't be disturbed,' Andrew pointed out, but he seemed to be resigned to doing what he was told.

He sat down heavily on the sofa and began to undo his shoes.

'Our cue to depart,' Belinda said with a giggle, and marched Nell out of the room. For her friend she had commandeered the bedroom next to hers, whose owner was away on holiday.

'Couldn't you have found another for Andrew?' Nell queried. 'He'd have been more comfortable in a proper bed.'

Belinda winked at her. 'There are two empty rooms, but if he'd been up here he'd have got ideas. Much better where he is! Or did you want him paying you a visit?' She ducked as Nell threw a sandal at her, laughed and said goodnight.

They left London at ten o'clock, after a leisurely breakfast. Andrew seemed to have recovered his usual good humour and was delighted to discover several acquaintances among the senior residents. Even the R.S.O., under whom Nell and Belinda had suffered, turned out to be an old friend of his.

'Good thing Ted's away for the weekend,' Belinda murmured under cover of the general chat, 'Though he's bound to hear about it.'

'I don't see why he should if you don't tell him.'

'Be your age, Nell! This place thrives on gossip.'

'Very true,' thought Nell. 'And perhaps all for the best.' It might discourage Ted, put him off visiting her. Such a pity they couldn't have remained what they had been through five years of medical school, good friends and nothing more.

Nell had a hard job dragging Andrew away from Q.C.H. Happily reminiscing about his own triumphs on the rugby field, he would have been quite content to stay for lunch. 'But I told my aunt I'd be back by midday.' Nell had telephoned early that morning in case they were worrying about her, and Elizabeth had said coolly that she would appreciate Nell's return because she wanted to go out after lunch. By common consent they never left the Colonel alone in the house.

'Does it matter when you're back?' Andrew asked off-handedly, and Nell told him that it did. 'Proper little kill-joy, aren't you?' he grumbled, but goodnaturedly today, because he had after all enjoyed himself, though perhaps not in the way that he had intended.

They reached Lanmore at half past twelve and were at the Manor two minutes later. They swung on to the fore-court to the noise of flying gravel, for Andrew was inclined to brake at the last possible moment. Nell saw Philip's Aston Martin parked beside her aunt's car, and as she climbed out of the red two-seater he came out of the front door accompanied by Elizabeth.

Elizabeth was immaculate as always, hair smooth and neatly coiled, elegantly dressed and smartly shod. She looked as if she had just returned from church and so did Philip. They made Nell feel self-conscious in the duffle coat and thick boots she had donned this morning for the return journey. She had a sudden absurd desire that Philip could have seen her last night in her borrowed finery, was annoyed at her own foolishness and rushed into speech as a result.

'Hallo, you two. We're back at last!' She ran a hand over her windblown curls, wishing she had the sort of hair that would look good in a chignon, as her aunt's did.

Elizabeth took in her niece's untidy appearance with one of those smiles that only just moved her lips, and turned to share an amused glance with Philip.

'Hope you weren't worried last night,' Nell rushed on. 'I'd have rung if it hadn't been so late when we decided to stay.'

They were all looking at her and Nell realised that she was talking too much. She swallowed and there was a little silence, broken by her aunt. 'That's quite all right, Nell. I guessed what had happened.' Something had put her in an exceptionally good mood this morning. Philip's company, possibly? 'Come in for a drink, Andrew,' she suggested, with more warmth than she usually showed towards him. 'I'll be with you as soon as I've seen Philip off.'

They were not going to Philip's house for lunch today, because they had a lot to do before the move tomorrow. When Elizabeth joined them she was looking very pleased with herself. Her manner towards Andrew was almost affable, and once she gave a little laugh as if she was enjoying some secret joke.

'Where's Grandpa?' Nell asked.

'Having a day in bed. Sandy thought he'd been over-doing it,' and at Nell's anxious look, 'No, he's all right. Sitting up reading the Sunday papers and grumbling about having to move tomorrow.'

Andrew left a few minutes later and Nell said she would finish off her drink in the old man's company. 'One moment, Nell!' Elizabeth held up a finger, and the girl halted in the doorway. 'I didn't tell him you were out all night. I thought it wiser not to.'

'Didn't tell him . . . why ever not?'

'Your grandfather's old-fashioned. He doesn't approve of the modern life-style.'

'Elizabeth! It was too late to come home and Andrew's blood alcohol must have been alarmingly high.' Nell smiled at the thought, then stopped smiling at her aunt's next words.

'You don't have to make excuses to me, Nell. You're of age. You can choose your own way of life,' and a thoroughly reprehensible way it is, her tone implied.

Nell would have done better to leave well alone, but she found it difficult to allow Elizabeth the last word. 'I don't see anything very terrible about spending the night in London.'

'Don't you, dear? With Andrew?' A wealth of meaning in those few words.

'If you want to know, Elizabeth, we stayed at Q.C.H. In the doctors' wing. Belle found me a bed, and I did not share it with Andrew.'

Her aunt's well-bred face registered disapproval and distaste. 'Really, Nell! Spare me the details. I am only concerned that you shouldn't upset your grandfather.'

'I don't think Grandpa would be upset by the truth!' snapped Nell. 'And unlike you, he'd probably believe me.'

'Would he, dear? Philip jumped to the obvious conclusion,' her aunt said smugly.

Nell gave her an astounded and angry stare. 'For crying out loud, why bring him into it?' and then she knew why her aunt had been in such a good mood when Andrew and she had arrived. She had been pleased that Philip had seen them together, and had undoubtedly made plain to him that they had been out all night. Cunning Aunt Elizabeth, disposing of the opposition! Though Nell doubted if Philip cared one way or the other how she spent her time. He had given her the most cursory of glances and she had avoided looking at him, because she had been selfconscious and gauche. Remembering her bright and meaningless remarks in the courtyard, Nell gave an angry laugh. They had thought she was ill at ease because of a guilty conscience, and not quite bold enough to carry it off with aplomb.

She topped up her glass with a hand that shook slightly, swallowed most of it at one gulp and went abruptly from the room.

Next morning the builders moved in and the family moved out. 'Whatever you say we're putting you to a lot of trouble,' Nell said worriedly as Philip showed her to her room. She had come round to his house later than the others, because she had waited to admit the workmen.

'Nonsense.' He stood in the bedroom doorway, unsmiling, and she wondered why he looked so grim.

'You do such a lot for us and we're not even very old friends.'

'You're very dear friends,' Philip said firmly, then made an amendment to that. 'Your grandfather and Elizabeth.'

'Well, naturally.' Nell said quickly, her colour mounting and her voice rather high, 'I don't look on myself as a friend.'

'Don't you, Nell?' His smile was difficult to read. 'How would you like to define our relationship, then?'

Her chest felt tight. It had been an abysmal error to come to this man's house. 'I wouldn't say we had a relationship,' she managed unsteadily, and he laughed unkindly.

'We could always develop one, or wouldn't Andrew care for that?'

'Why bring him into it?' Nell asked stormily.

'You know why.'

'Andrew's just a friend. Oh, for goodness' sake, Philip, this is a ridiculous conversation!'

He ignored her last remark. 'Rather an intimate friend,' he said sardonically, 'if you spend the night with him.'

'Oh, stop it! You're as bad as Elizabeth. I thought it was only women who indulged in gossip.'

'My dear Nell,' he said cuttingly, 'I am not in the least interested in your love life. You can be as promiscuous as a cat for all I care, but I don't like to see your family upset. Couldn't you be more ... discreet?'

'There's nothing to be discreet about!'

'If you say so.' He sounded bored and disbelieving. 'Come down when you're ready. The others are having coffee.'

'I knew it was a mistake to come here,' Nell muttered at his departing back, but she didn't think he heard, or if he did he paid no attention. 'I don't care what you think,' she announced, and pushed the door to with a bang. Childish behaviour, but Philip's readiness to condemn pricked at her composure. From the expertise of his lovemaking he had had plenty of practice, so what right had he to criticise? And what exactly had he meant by those remarks about their relationship? There had been a sort of amused contempt in his voice, as if he no longer had any respect for her. Nell didn't care to examine too closely why this should upset her so much.

She determined to keep out of Philip's way as much as possible, so she was delighted when Dr MacFarlane asked her to do some extra sessions at the surgery. Andrew was attending a three-day symposium on heart disease in Birmingham, and Nell agreed to do every morning while he was away, plus one evening surgery.

'And why can't I be on call on Thursday night?' she asked eagerly. 'It is your off duty time.'

Dr Mac's expression was dubious. 'Sure you feel up to it?'

'Of course I do.' Nell stifled a pang of apprehension at the thought that it would be the first time she was totally on her own. Perhaps the shrewd old doctor read her mind, for he gave her a pat on the shoulder and pointed out that he would be around if she was desperate. He had no plans to be out that night.

As Nell drove home from the surgery she pondered the problem of her future. She got on so well with the MacFarlanes. She could finish off her training with them. Belinda and Jimmy, however, had other views on the subject and thought she would be crazy to accept.

'Throwing away your chances!'

'Stagnating in the country!'

'Hey, am I stagnating?' Andrew had asked indignantly, and they had said that was different. He had finished his training, held a whole lot more hospital posts than Nell had done.

It was a difficult decision and she had to give an answer to Dr MacFarlane by the end of the month. She was still frowning over her thoughts when she reached Philip's house, to find a strange car in the drive. To her surprise and dismay it was Ted's. He had driven down from London on the offchance of finding her in, and the builders had told him where she was staying.

'I knew you'd only put me off again if I told you I was coming,' he said, sounding defensive and very unsure of himself. Though she wasn't pleased to see him, Nell hadn't the heart to be cross with him. Thank heavens, she thought, that Philip had gone away. She felt a little uncomfortable asking Ted to lunch in someone else's house, but she had offered to be on call until two o'clock, so that Dr Mac could do his rounds in peace and have an undisturbed meal.

'A sort of trial run for my night on call,' she had suggested, and the old man had agreed.

'We could go somewhere local and you could leave their number with the surgery,' Ted suggested, but Nell told him there was nowhere good to eat within easy reach.

'I'd settle for a ploughman's lunch in the local pub,' he muttered, for his first meeting with Elizabeth and Colonel Whitehead had been decidedly strained. It was a stiff and uncomfortable meal, with poor Ted overawed by Elizabeth's cool dignity, and quite plainly terrified by the irascible old man.

'He isn't as bad as you seem to think,' Nell told him as they walked by the river later in the afternoon.

'No? You've forgotten very quickly how badly he treated you.' Ted hurled a fallen branch into the water and stood to watch Paddy plunge after it.

He was right; she had put the past behind her. No good came of brooding over old injustices. 'And some of the blame was on my side,' Nell mused. 'I should have been more tactful, tried harder to make it up.'

'I can see you've been thoroughly brainwashed,' Ted exclaimed disgustedly. 'Belinda says you're thinking quite seriously of staying on with these G.P.s.'

'Yes, I am.' Nell called Paddy to her and he lolloped up the bank, dripping wet and muddy. 'I'm not ambitious, Ted. I could be quite happy in general practice.'

'All right, but do some more house jobs first.' Ted had his own career meticulously planned. He knew what he would be doing two years from now. Nell admired his determination but lacked the incentive to emulate it. Only a few exceptional women were prepared to struggle like that. She had put her career before her family in the past, and it had not led to happiness.

'I suppose you've been influenced by this MacFarlane chap. Belle told me about him.' Ted's fair face flushed as he spoke.

Nell shook her head. 'If anything Andrew's being in the practice makes me less likely to accept.' At his sceptical look she tried to explain. 'It could be awkward working with him.'

'Because you're in love with him?' Ted cut in, and caught her by the arms and swung her round to face him.

'No, because he's a bit of a wolf,' Nell answered, trying for the light touch, for Ted in this difficult and possessive mood wasn't easy to handle.

'You haven't answered my question,' he persisted doggedly. 'Are you in love with him?'

'Oh, Ted, of course I'm not! I like him. I admire him as a doctor, but that's all.'

'I wish I could believe you.' His grip tightened on her arms, hurting her, for he was a powerful young man and at this moment under great emotional stress. 'Come back to London,' he said thickly. 'I miss you like hell.'

'Let me go, Ted!' Nell tried vainly to free herself.

He shook his head obstinately. 'If there's no one else then I've still got a chance,' and he lowered his head to hers.

He was a presentable young man, athletic, decent,

genuinely fond of her, and he moved Nell not at all. There was no spark between them. She stayed passive in his arms and after a few moments he let her go with a sigh. 'What is it about you, Nell? Are you frigid or something?'

A man's first assumption when he failed to arouse a woman, Nell thought wryly, and wondered how he would have felt if he could have seen her in Philip's arms. Why did one always have to be physically attracted to the wrong man, and why, oh, why did she have to keep on thinking about him?

'Let's go back,' she suggested. 'It must be nearly teatime.'

'I don't want another meal with your snooty relatives,' said Ted, sounding like a sulky schoolboy. 'Your grandfather may improve on acquaintance, but your aunt is a right bitch.'

They walked along in a heavy silence, the dogs the only cheerful members of the party. At the house Ted stopped by his car. 'I might as well go back. No point in staying.' He looked very young and unhappy, so that Nell's kind heart was troubled.

'Please stay to tea. It's such a long journey back. I'm ... truly sorry to have disappointed you.'

He made a brave attempt at a smile. 'I believe you. I suppose I've been a fool, expecting a girl from your sort of background to fall for a chap like me.'

'That's an idiotic thing to say!' Nell slipped an arm through his. 'Come and have tea or I'll think you're afraid to face Aunt Elizabeth again!'

The housekeeper had already wheeled in the tea trolley. They were eating in the main sitting-room, which was a pity, because the smaller room was cosier and more friendly. It was also unfortunate, from Nell's point of view, to find Philip already returned from his business trip earlier than expected. He made her edgy, so that she was less able to give Ted the moral support the young man needed. Ted sat beside Colonel Whitehead, perspiring and unhappy, while the old man barked questions at him in a heavy-handed attempt to be friendly.

Nell sat on her grandfather's other side, facing Elizabeth and Philip, who chatted quietly together, though they looked in her direction now and then. Elizabeth's expression was supercilious. She quite plainly despised Ted's lack of social graces. Philip? Nell caught him eyeing the young doctor with a look that was almost pitying. Then his gaze shifted to her again and became disagreeably sardonic, so that she turned away quickly and began talking to the other two.

Tea was nearly as much of an ordeal for Nell as for Ted, so that when he leant forward and gave her a despairing look, she interpreted it correctly. 'Get me out of here! I can't stand much more of this!'

'Ted has to get away,' she announced, and he rose with alacrity. He was too pleased to be going to prolong the farewells.

'Don't make a hasty decision,' he urged, leaning out of the car window with an earnest and worried look. 'Once you cut yourself off from your teaching hospital it's not easy getting back.'

'It's hard to believe that young man is a doctor,' Elizabeth observed, when Nell returned to the room.

'Why?' Nell asked sharply, and her aunt shrugged.

'Those manners, my dear! No poise at all. I'm astonished that he was accepted for training.'

'He was accepted because he did brilliantly in his A-levels. He's not usually so awkward. You made him nervous, all of you, sitting there looking so superior.'

'Nonsense, nonsense,' rumbled the Colonel. 'Did my best to make the fellow feel at home.'

'Oh, Grandpa!' Nell's ill humour dissolved into helpless laughter. 'Asking him what the hunting was like round his way! He comes from Liverpool!'

'And how was I to know that, miss?' the Colonel

snapped though his lips twitched in sympathy.

Nell excused herself and departed, because she had an evening surgery. She felt unsettled by Ted's visit and by his last words. Should she stay? Should she go? Her grandfather would miss her, but her aunt would be glad.

The surgery was a long one. There were more problems than usual, social as well as medical. Struggling to find a hospital bed for an old woman who wasn't desperately ill, but who yet needed some attention, Nell began to wonder if her friends weren't right, that she ought to have more training. She was still too young and unsure of herself to handle difficult house physicians.

'If it's only a minor stroke surely she can be looked after at home?' the resident doctor urged, and Nell gripped the receiver tightly and hung on to her temper.

'I've already told you, she's eighty and she lives alone.'

'Family? Friends?'

'Her cottage is two miles from another house.'

'Heard of district nurses, doctor?' The cocky young voice at the other end of the line fired Nell to indignation.

'They don't provide an all-night service. If it was your mother would you like the thought of her, on her own up a cart track, without even a telephone?' That silenced him and the old lady was accepted.

'As a temporary measure only,' the house physician warned. 'We're hard pressed for beds, so the sooner you can work something out with the social services the better.'

He was only doing his duty, trying to keep his scarce beds for acutely ill patients. Nell couldn't blame him, though she resented the time she had spent in trying to convince him.

'You look tired, doctor. I'll fix up the ambulance,' Miss Winter offered. She was a tower of strength. Nell thanked her gratefully and said that she would call on Mrs Hayes on her way home. She had visited the old lady that morning for the routine once-monthly checkup that Dr Mac-

Farlane insisted all his oldest patients should have, and discovered her with speech slightly slurred and one arm out of action, the little cottage chaotic, the bed unmade. Mrs Hayes had been nearly as reluctant as the houseman over admission, but she had had several hours to think about it, and to dread the approaching night.

She welcomed Nell with open relief, and because she was apprehensive about a new experience, Nell sat with her until the ambulance came. 'You see, doctor,' Mrs Hayes explained, 'I've never been in hospital. All my children were born here,' and she raised a thin old hand to point waveringly at the ceiling.

How times had changed! No modern doctor would consider delivering babies in this remote cottage, without even a piped water supply. Nell spared a thought for the courage and dedication of those old-time G.P.s, and wondered if her generation would ever be their equal.

CHAPTER EIGHT

By the time she reached Philip's house the others had finished their evening meal, and were having coffee. Nell had telephoned to say she might be held up, but hadn't expected to be so late.

'I'm terribly sorry,' she said awkwardly.

Elizabeth glanced at the dainty French clock on the mantelpiece and shook her head reprovingly. 'Must your surgery go on quite so long? It is a bit inconvenient for Philip.'

Nell coloured and took the drink that Philip put into her hand. 'You look as though you need a pick-me-up,' he commented quite kindly. 'And Elizabeth, Nell can't help being late. Doctors don't keep nine-to-five hours, after all.'

'But your housekeeper may not like having to serve meals at this hour.'

'Mrs Reed is the last woman to make a fuss, especially when she knows there's a good reason.'

He was correct in this. Mrs Reed brushed aside Nell's apologies with a smile. 'Can't be helped, doctor. And Mr Trent's away so much that we have an easy time of it most of the year.'

Nell had reached the dessert stage and was tucking in to apple pie when Philip walked in. 'All right?'

'Yes, thank you,' she said politely.

He sat down opposite her. 'You looked a bit fraught just now. Don't let Elizabeth's remarks upset you.'

She concentrated on her pie. 'Yes, but I do keep odd hours. It might be better if I stayed with the MacFarlanes. Andrew thinks so.'

'I'll bet he does, but your grandfather wouldn't like

it. They're two men on their own, and when Sandy's out there would be just you and Andrew.' His expression was sardonic. 'Do you enjoy playing them off against each other?'

'I don't know what you're talking about.'

'You know perfectly well what I'm talking about! That lad looked pretty despondent.'

'You saw how it was at tea,' Nell said quickly.

'The effect of your family? I expect that made it worse, but I should have said'—he gave her a hard unsmiling look—'that the poor young man had been rebuffed.'

He was altogether too perceptive. Nell pressed her lips together and took a deep breath, determined not to start an argument. Her colour rose under his ironic gaze. Her self-control slipped and she burst out angrily, 'Why don't you go away!' recalled that he was after all her host, and mumbled a sort of apology.

'Coffee in the drawing-room,' he remarked, ignoring both outburst and apology, and walked out of the room. As if she was a toddler, Nell thought indignantly, turning on tantrums which were better ignored.

'I have some notes to write up,' she announced to his departing back. 'I don't want any coffee.'

This incident strengthened her determination to move from Philip's house as soon as possible. Next morning she called at the Manor to see what the workmen were doing. She picked her way through plaster, tripped over a ladder, and received a disapproving stare from the foreman.

'This really isn't the place for you, miss. Live here? It's impossible,' and looking at the total chaos around her, Nell was forced to agree. Today was going to be a busy one. She would decide what to do after Andrew came back.

That night she had her first taste of how exhausting a G.P.'s life could be. Dr MacFarlane had insisted on taking the evening surgery, so that she could have supper in peace.

She was drinking coffee and leafing through one of Philip's books when the telephone rang.

It was for her—a farm labourer's wife, saying that her husband had vomited blood. The men were playing chess, but Elizabeth kept her eyes on Nell's face while her niece was speaking. 'All right, Mrs Thomas, I'll be with you as soon as possible. Keep him warm. Keep him flat, and keep calm if you possibly can.'

And the same went for her, she thought, as she turned right at the top of Philip's drive. She had to appear calm when she saw Mr Thomas, even if she was a mass of nerves underneath. This was her first real emergency outside a hospital. At Q.C.H., backed up by the casualty staff, with senior doctors just around the corner, any well trained person could cope. Here she was on her own.

An hour later, as the ambulance drove off with Mr Thomas and his wife, Nell felt a sense of achievement and quiet confidence. When she had walked into the house there had been an uncomfortable feeling in the pit of her stomach, a sudden apprehension that she might be out of her depth. However, as soon as she saw Mr Thomas, ashen-faced from blood loss and quite plainly terrified, she forgot her own doubts and fears in the need to remove his. She had not disgraced her teachers. She had not needed to tele-phone Dr MacFarlane. Next time would be easier, because nothing could ever be as bad as your first emergency.

Nell drove back to Philip's in a mood of near-euphoria, parked her car near the front door and walked into the drawing-room. The chess game was over and only her family were in the room.

'You're looking very pleased with yourself,' her grand-father commented, and her aunt, after a critical stare, asked if she actually enjoyed seeing people ill.

'Of course I don't, but it is nice to help them. To know that you can.' She gave a smile as she remembered the grati-tude in Mrs Thomas' eyes and the woman's last words.

'We weren't frightened any more after you came.'

Elizabeth shrugged. 'Each man to his taste, I suppose. And woman too! *I* couldn't do it.' She returned to her book.

Her aunt's words deflated Nell, so that the mood of euphoria evaporated and she realised how tired she was. Ten o'clock! 'Time for bed, Grandpa!' They had talked the old man into retiring early as a regular habit. He embarked on his customary grumble, to which Nell listened indulgently.

'Wish I could go to bed, but I'll probably be called out again.'

'No life for a young girl,' the Colonel growled as they crossed the hall together. 'Don't like the thought of you wandering round the countryside in the middle of the night.'

Hearing their voices, Philip came out of his study, swinging a pair of spectacles in one hand. He told Nell that he agreed with her grandfather. 'Take one of the dogs with you.' Paddy and Ranger had moved with the family, though Elizabeth had decreed that they must stay in one of the outhouses.

'All right,' Nell answered. 'It's a good idea.'

They said goodnight to the old man, and as he climbed the stairs slowly Philip lingered in the hall. 'It's not often you agree with me, my girl.' There was a glint in his eyes as he looked down at her.

Nell stepped back a few paces, because he was having his usual effect on her, and however hard she tried she could not be indifferent to him. Physical attraction was a mysterious business. Her head told her that she disliked him; her senses told her quite otherwise. She made a light rejoinder and followed her grandfather upstairs, conscious that Philip was still standing in the hall watching her, with that ironic little half-smile that made her want to hit him.

He knew just how he affected her, damn him! He might

even kiss her again if he felt in the mood, and if she had an
ounce of self-respect she would rebuff him. Make it plain
that she was not as he believed her to be, that she was not
the sort of girl whom men labelled easy.

Her aunt went to bed at eleven, remarking wistfully that
she hadn't realised Philip worked so hard. He had been
shut in his study all evening, and when Nell went out to
answer another call he was still there. The curtains weren't
drawn and she could see him, hunched over his desk, totally absorbed in whatever he was doing. To her surprise
the light was still on when she returned at two in the morning. Paddy showed unusually great reluctance to enter his
shed, dropping himself heavily to the ground and refusing
to budge.

'You great fat lump! Move!' Nell panted, heaving at
him angrily. He licked her hand but stayed where he was.

'What are you trying to do?' came Philip's voice from
the darkness.

'Trying to get him back into the shed.'

'Bring him into the house. Ranger too,' for the other
Labrador was keeping up a persistent whine from behind
the shut door.

'Oh, thank you, Philip. They're very offended at being
shut up out here.'

'Then why do it?' he enquired as they walked back to the
house, the delighted dogs bounding beside them.

'Elizabeth said that if I insisted on bringing them I was
to keep them out of your way. She thought they should
have gone to the vet's.'

'To the vet's! For six weeks?'

'Yes, I know, but Elizabeth doesn't like dogs. She says
you don't either.'

'Your aunt has the wrong idea about a lot of things,' he
retorted, sounding faintly irritated, opened the front door
for her and followed her into the hall. 'The only reason I
don't keep dogs myself is because I'm away so much, and

it hardly seems fair to make more work for the Reeds.'

'Do you often work this late?' asked Nell, thinking that he looked a lot fresher than she felt.

He shrugged. 'When the need arises. I get most of my best ideas at night. Come and warm yourself in the study and I'll bring you a hot drink.'

Touched by this thoughtfulness, Nell walked into his room, where a log fire still burnt brightly, the one touch of homeliness in a strictly functional room. The shelves were lined by books on physics and electronics, papers covered with calculations and diagrams lay scattered on his desk. A large piece of cartridge paper was pinned to a work bench, beside it a metal ruler and calculator. She sat down on a stool in front of the fire, thinking how little she really knew about Philip. This was his work, the world of applied science, and when he retreated into it he became another man, as her aunt seemed to be discovering with some dismay.

'I shouldn't be disturbing you when you're so busy,' she apologised as he came back with two mugs of Ovaltine and the remains of a fruit cake.

He hitched himself on to the corner of his big desk. 'I've finished for the night. I was thinking of stopping when I heard your car.'

He had shut the study door and Nell was conscious of their isolation in the quiet dark house. She kept her eyes on the fire, and ate the cake he cut for her, though for some ridiculous reason she seemed to have difficulty in swallowing.

'Nell?' He spoke from just behind her and she swung round sharply, startled because she hadn't heard him get off the desk. The only light was from the fire and a small table lamp. He looked enormous and somehow menacing, though his face was in shadow. She backed away from him, and he gave an angry laugh.

'Do you have to behave so ridiculously?' He moved towards her again and she stepped back into the wall. He swore softly under his breath, and as a log flared it cast a flickering light on to his face. Nell could see in those brief seconds that he was very angry. His eyes glittered and his mouth was compressed. He put one hand on each side of her, so that she couldn't move away, and gazed down at her.

'Don't look at me like that. I'm fed up to the back teeth with the way you've behaved ever since you've come to stay —most of the time, anyhow.' Astounded, she could only gape at him. 'Avoiding me as much as possible, stiff as a poker when you can't. What are you afraid of, Nell? That I'll kiss you again? I shouldn't have thought that a girl of your experience would bother about that.' He brought out the last words contemptuously, flicked her cheek with a hard finger and moved away.

There was an unpleasant lump in Nell's throat. She swallowed painfully. 'If you dislike me so much, why did you insist on my coming to stay? And why invite me in here tonight? You didn't have to, after all.'

He threw himself into the easy chair on the other side of the fire. 'Good question,' he agreed moodily, 'and no easy answer. You're a very ... desirable girl, Nell ... will that do for a start?'

Her mouth felt dry. Her heart was beating very hard. Philip wanted her, and was furious with himself because of it. Or with her. Or with both of them. Wanted her, but hadn't said a word about loving, or even liking. 'I'm going away again tomorrow,' he added into the small silence. 'I shall be on the Continent for a fortnight or so. I think it might be better if you find somewhere else to stay before I get back.'

Pride kept Nell's head high, helped her to walk to the door with a measure of composure. 'I agree with you,' she managed, but couldn't quite bring herself to look at him.

'If you remember I never wanted to come here in the first place.'

Then she was out of the study and running across the hall, taking the stairs two at a time, her breath coming in great gasps, until she reached the privacy of her room and could throw herself on to the bed. She lay face down, dry-eyed but despairing. She knew now why Philip disturbed her so profoundly. She was in love with him, had been for a long time, though she had fought against admitting it.

She didn't think she had given herself away, because that would have been the ultimate humiliation—to expose her emotions to a man who wanted only one thing from her. If she hadn't been a guest in his house—correction, if her grandfather hadn't been here as well, he would have made love to her tonight. But he respected and liked the old man, and could hardly betray him by sleeping with his grand-daughter. So he had asked her to go, because the tension between them was becoming intolerable. He found her a distraction, and it was an experience he didn't like.

Desolately Nell remembered something Pamela Middleton-Massey had once said, 'He has girl-friends scattered all over Europe!' He wouldn't waste any time thinking about her once he was away. She was just the irritating girl of whom he had never really approved, and whom he now thoroughly disliked, because she disturbed his peace of mind. Nell pushed herself up on the bed and fumbled for the light switch so that she could undress, pray-ing she wouldn't be called out again tonight. Her head ached so violently that it would be difficult to think clearly, if she had to make a decision. In the morning she would go round to the surgery and ask Dr MacFarlane if she could stay with them for the next few weeks. At the same time she would tell him that she had made up her mind about the job. She couldn't possibly work in this neigh-bourhood. She wanted to get as far away from Philip as possible, though she was bound to meet him occasionally, when she came home for weekends. Calmer now that she had made this decision, Nell snapped the light off and shut her aching eyes.

She slept late in the morning and arrived downstairs to find only one place laid at the dining table. She hurried to the kitchen, full of apologies, which Mrs Reed brushed aside.

'Mr Trent told me you were up half the night, doctor. I'll bring your breakfast now. What would you like?'

'I'm really not hungry. Could I just have a cup of coffee in here with you?'

They were sitting at the kitchen table, chatting companionably, when Mrs Reed remembered Philip's letter. She produced it from her apron pocket. 'He asked me to give you this. Said he didn't want to disturb you so early in the morning.'

Nell took the letter, but didn't open it. 'What time did he leave?'

'Seven o'clock. He had to drive to London Airport.'

And he had still been up at two in the morning. Nell rubbed her heavy eyes and wondered how he managed it. 'How long have you worked for Mr Trent?' she asked.

Mrs Reed smiled reminiscently. 'Five years now, and my Joe had been out of work for nearly that long when Mr Trent took us on. He's a wonderful employer. Ask anyone who works for him, miss. The men on the farm feel just like we do.'

'I believe you,' said Nell, thinking sadly that Philip seemed to be kind to everyone but her. She fingered the letter and opened it when Mrs Reed rose to get more coffee.

Just a brief note written in a strong slanting hand: 'I behaved badly last night. I hope you'll accept my apologies. Of course there's no need for you to go. Please stay, at

least until I get back,
Philip.'

She was tempted, but stuck to her original decision. If she stayed she would only suffer further heartache. When she spoke to Dr MacFarlane he agreed that it would be easier if she lived in the village. His house was next door to the surgery. If she wanted to pick up notes on a patient before visiting them it would save time.

Andrew made some joke about having a pretty girl in the house, took in Nell's pale unhappy face and was suddenly quiet. When they were alone together he asked her what was wrong.

Nell shook her head. 'Please, Andrew, I'd rather not talk about it.'

He looked unusually sober. 'Something to do with that chap who came down from London recently?' At her surprised look he gave her a wry grin. 'Place like this you can't hide a thing.' He laid a hand on her shoulder, gave it a little squeeze. 'Cheer up, Nell. Your family agree to the move?'

'They can see the point. Elizabeth certainly approves. She thought I was a nuisance, keeping such erratic hours.'

'And the master of the house?'

Nell was quick to catch the disapproval in his voice, knowing that the two men didn't like each other. 'Philip?' She gave a brittle laugh. 'Even more pleased than Elizabeth to see me go, I'm sure.'

For the letter, she had decided, meant nothing. A polite gesture made more out of respect for her grandfather than because he was genuinely sorry for his behaviour.

Nell was even more deeply involved in surgery life now that she lived on the spot. Though she visited her grandfather every day, he complained that she was cutting herself off from them, and so in a way she was—immersing herself in medical work so that she had little time for brooding, helping Andrew collect data for an article he hoped to submit to the *British Medical Journal*, listening to Dr Mac's stories of his early days in the practice, when he had been no older than Nell was now.

'Such a pity you've decided to go back to London,' the old man observed one evening. 'You fit in so well, my dear. It's not too late to change your mind. I haven't sent off an advertisement yet.'

Nell gave him a warm smile. 'I'm touched, Dr Mac, but I really feel I should get more experience. Midwifery, paediatrics, perhaps E.N.T. Then I might apply for a trainee post, and if yours is free . . .' She let the words trail off, wondering if in a couple of years, when the wounds had healed, she might be prepared to come back.

'But by that time there may be no reason for you to work here,' the doctor observed, and Nell stared at him.

'Why not?'

'Your grandfather may be gone.'

Apprehension gripped her. 'Are you trying to tell me something? Isn't he doing as well as he was?'

'He's eighty, my dear child, and we all have to die some time.' At her stricken face he sighed. 'You're very fond of him, aren't you? I've never understood why you didn't make it up sooner.'

'I tried to,' Nell told him, blinking away the tears that stung her eyes. 'I wrote several times, but he never answered. I rang, but Elizabeth told me he didn't want to speak to me.'

The doctor's expression was thoughtful. 'He never told me that. I always thought he was too proud to make the first move, but would have welcomed one from you.'

'Well, he didn't,' Nell said shortly. 'And I don't think he wants to go over it now. So please, Dr Mac, let's respect his wishes and not rake over the past. And by the way, I'm not looking for jobs in London, but somewhere in this region. Birmingham maybe, or Westhampton. There's a good hospital there.'

The two weeks since Philip had gone were almost over. 'He comes back tomorrow,' Colonel Whitehead said, when Nell had tea with him the following day. The thought gave her a sleepless night. She couldn't avoid seeing him, because she would have to visit her grandfather, unless the old man came round to the MacFarlanes' house. She could plead pressure of work and with any luck Philip might be off again in a few days, so that she would have a little longer before she had to meet him. It was cowardly and foolish and only a postponement, but it would give her a chance to recover her equilibrium. At the moment she had a humiliating tendency to dissolve into tears under stress.

Dr MacFarlane was delighted to see his old friend, whom he was no longer visiting as a patient.

'So come again tomorrow,' Nell urged. 'Good for you to get out, Grandpa, and I am rather busy.' Mr Reed had driven the Colonel and would be calling back for him at six o'clock. When she walked out to the car with him Nell managed a casual, 'Philip back?'

The old man nodded.

'Is he staying long?'

'Couldn't say,' and with that she had to be content.

After a second visit from her grandfather Andrew said thoughtfully, 'What are you up to, Nell? Why don't you want to go to Trent's house?' He stared at her bent head. 'You're not that busy, so what's keeping you away?'

A half truth would be easier than complete evasion. 'Philip and I—we don't get on——'

'So that's why you wanted to come here. I did wonder. But you have to see him some time. Aren't you being a bit childish?'

'I expect I am,' Nell agreed bitterly. 'But if I never saw him again it would suit me.' She realised from Andrew's expression that she was reacting too violently and stopped abruptly, her colour high. If he read more into her words than she wanted him to, he kept it to himself, though he looked very thoughtful as he went out of the room.

Nell was pottering in the garden the following afternoon, dead-heading the MacFarlanes' tulips, when she heard a car crunch to a halt on the gravel. She walked round the side of the house, expecting to see her grandfather's Rover, but came to an abrupt halt when she saw Philip's car. He stepped out of it, slammed the door and stalked towards her, grim-faced.

She swallowed nervously. 'Well, hallo! I wasn't expecting to see you.'

'Your grandfather is feeling rather tired today. I persuaded him not to come.'

'Oh. Did he send a message?'

'He hopes you'll come back with me. However busy you are.' This with sarcasm.

The blood hammered in Nell's ears so that she found it difficult to think straight, so startled was she by his unexpected appearance. She was behaving like an idiot and he thought so too—that much was apparent from his contemptuous expression. 'Come on, girl,' he said under his breath.

'I'm not dressed for visiting.' She looked down at her jeans and sweater, at the shabby suede shoes on her feet.

He gave them a cursory glance. 'You look all right to me. Come on!'

'But why in your car? I'll follow in mine.'

'No, you won't.' He took her arm in a hard grip. 'I've a few things to say to you. In private. The car's the best place for that.'

Short of a scene on the drive, which might be overheard by passers-by in the lane, Nell had no choice but to go with him. Besides, she felt too low in spirits to resist. It was shattering to discover how helpless she was to control her

emotions. How powerful a hold the mind had on the body!
This man, who looked at her with such dislike, had made
her knees tremble and her hands shake. When she fumbled
at the car door, he opened it impatiently and waved her in.

They turned off the village green, drove a short distance
towards Philip's house and swung on to a grass verge, under
some trees. Nell stared blindly through the windscreen
and waited for him to speak.

'You got the letter I wrote? Before I went away?'

'Yes, I did.'

'Then why didn't you stay?'

'Because I wanted to go.'

'I see.' He said it softly, reaching into the glove compartment for cigarettes, taking his time over lighting up.
'So you haven't forgiven me?'

'No, I haven't!' exclaimed Nell, suddenly as angry as he
was. 'You made it too plain I was only there on sufferance.
That you only asked me to stay because of Grandpa.'

'Did I say that?'

'You didn't need to.' She rolled her window down and
took a deep breath of the sweet spring air. 'Please drive on,
Philip,' she said wearily. 'I suppose it was silly trying to
avoid you.'

'Very silly, since you were bound to meet me before
long.' He threw his cigarette out of the window, but still
he didn't turn on the engine. 'You know why we can't get
on, don't you?' he asked abruptly, and she looked away
quickly, her heart beating fast.

It was between them again, however she might deny it,
the fierce pull of an intense physical attraction. When he
put his hand on the nape of her neck her breath came
faster. 'Oh, Philip!' She turned into his arms, clung blindly
to him and returned his kisses with passion.

There was the sound of a car in the distance and they
drew apart just as it reached the bend in the road. Philip
waited for it to pass, then turned the ignition key. 'I didn't

mean that to happen,' he said evenly, 'but you have a way
of looking at a man ... those big brown eyes and those
tumbled curls ... very sexy, as I'm sure you must know.'

It wasn't intended as a compliment, and Nell's face
whitened. 'Why do you dislike me so much, Philip? What
have I ever done to you?'

'Got under my skin. Taken my mind off my work,' he
said savagely.

'But if ... if we feel the same way ... and you must
know that I do ...' She stumbled to a halt, intimidated by
his scornful expression.

'What are you offering me, Nell? An affair? Under your
grandfather's nose? I couldn't do it to the old man. Besides, I don't care to share you with Andrew, or have you
finished with him already?' He put the car into gear and
rolled forward off the grass.

'I've told you about Andrew——'

'So you have, only I don't believe you. Very convenient
for you, living in his house. Especially when the old man's
out at night.' The words were insulting, his tone even more
so.

'I give up,' Nell said bitterly. 'You're cruel and intolerant and—and the most hateful man I've ever met!'

'You have a nasty temper, little Nell.' He had recovered
his control completely and it put her at a disadvantage.
'Simmer down before we reach the house or everyone will
know we've been quarrelling. I have visitors,' he added as
they drew up at his front door. 'Friends from Stockholm.'

They were all on the terrace at the back of the house,
enjoying the warmest day of the year, her grandfather and
Elizabeth, James Fenton and his young sister, and the visitors from Sweden. Herr Petersen was a stocky grey-haired
man of no particular distinction, with a strikingly beautiful
daughter. As they shook hands Nell was all too conscious of
the contrast between Ilse Petersen's trendy suede suit and
her own much washed sweater and jeans. It made her awk-

ward and more abrupt than usual, especial as Philip was right beside her, performing the introductions with smooth urbanity.

As soon as she could she moved away from them, drew up a chair by her grandfather and asked quietly how he was.

He did appear tired. There was a pinched look about his nose and more of a tremor to his hands than usual. 'Feeling my age today,' he admitted, and this was so unlike him that Nell felt very concerned. However, he would hate a public discussion on his health, so she held her peace for the moment and left him to drowse in the sun.

James Fenton brought her a cup of tea and Bobbie dropped into the chair on her other side. 'What do you think of the beautiful Ilse?' she asked under her breath.

Nell looked along the terrace to where Ilse talked alone with Philip, her chair drawn close to his, her blonde hair a striking contrast to her deeply tanned face. When they had shaken hands she had topped Nell by a head. She was a big girl, beautifully proportioned, with the grace of an athlete and the face of a film star.

'Quite something,' Nell said lightly. 'She makes me feel ... inadequate.'

Bobbie gave a dramatic sigh. 'Me too. And she's not just good to look at. James says she's a rising young interior deocrator, highly regarded in Stockholm. *And* she's a champion skier. No point competing with all that!'

'None at all,' agreed James, 'But why do you want to?'

Bobbie gave him an aggrieved look. 'You know why. If I could make Philip realise that I'm no longer a little girl!'

'He won't as long as you make silly remarks like that,' James said severely, but his expression was indulgent as he looked at his young sister. 'Personally,' he observed, transferring his gaze to Nell, 'I find perfect women rather intimidating. She looks like Brünnhilde. To be admired from afar!'

Nell had to laugh. 'You're absolutely right. She's just like a Wagner heroine,' but behind the laughter she felt the ache of despair. How intimate was Philip with this beautiful woman? How often did he meet her in his travels abroad?

She found out from Herr Petersen when they were strolling on the lawn after tea. 'Ilse loves this place,' he told Nell with an affectionate glance at his daughter, where she still sat on the terrace with Philip. 'It is always a pleasure for us to come here.'

'You've been often?'

'Not often. Three—no, four times,' Herr Petersen replied in his precise English. 'And Philip as often to us. He stays with us when he is in Sweden. He has a lot in common with Ilse, I think—both so talented and so ambitious. I understand you are also a career woman, Dr Ramsay.'

'I do have a career,' Nell agreed with a little sigh. 'But I don't think I'm really a career woman.'

'Is it not then the same?' Herr Petersen asked, frowning over the distinction.

There was one, thought Nell, though it was too subtle to explain to a stranger and a foreigner at that. She loved her work but was not ambitious. She wanted only to be a good doctor. She wasn't one of those women who set their sights on a consultant post, and were prepared to sacrifice almost anything to get there. In her student days Nell had vaguely envisaged a future in which she might have a husband and a part-time medical practice. She was too feminine to want to compete full-time in a medical world that was still dominated by men. However, she had to earn a living, and that dream of marriage had disappeared entirely, swept away by the reality of her feelings for Philip. She had told him he was hateful, wild words that meant nothing. She loved him and longed to be in Ilse's place. She had been cut to the heart by the easy camaraderie between him and the Swedish girl.

She had never at any time been on those sort of terms with Philip, nor was ever likely to be, judging by their recent interlude. Philip's admiration for the Swedish girl was there for all to see. Respect? She probably had that too. Love? Not yet, surely, or he would not have behaved to Nell as he had done in the car. That was small comfort, however, for physical passion without tenderness was a cruel and comfortless thing.

James drove her back to the MacFarlanes'. Philip, engrossed in conversation with the Petersens, hardly noticed her departure. Elizabeth, who had been very quiet all through tea, decided to come with them.

'It's ages since I've had a talk with Sandy, and he's off duty this evening.'

Although there was no liking between them, Nell felt very sorry for her aunt. Elizabeth had looked her age on the terrace in the bright spring sunshine. Elegance and breeding could not compete with the splendour of Ilse's youth and beauty.

CHAPTER NINE

NEXT morning there was a letter for Nell, asking her to attend for interview the following week at Westhampton Royal Infirmary.

'You know Mr Trent has just opened a factory there?' Mrs. Reed asked, when Nell took the letter into the kitchen to show her.

This news was very unwelcome. 'No, I didn't,' Nell said slowly. 'I remember James Fenton mentioning some town in the Midlands. I don't think he said which one.'

She went out of the kitchen with a heavy heart, her pleasure at being selected for an interview quite gone. Was her peace of mind to be disturbed wherever she went? Would she never get away from thoughts of Philip? 'Snap out of it!' she told herself firmly. 'Stop being so childish!' For Westhampton was a large town, almost a city, and the chance of running into Philip there was very small. *If* she got the job, which was by no means certain.

She did get it, rather to her surprise, for there were three other applicants at the interview, all of whom seemed cleverer and more sure of themselves than she was. It was a step up from her last post as a house surgeon, for her appointment was as senior house officer in obstetrics, to commence on May the fourteenth.

'Is that too soon?' she asked Dr MacFarlane. 'I don't want to leave you in the lurch.'

In his blunt way he told her that they had managed without her before and could again. 'Though I've already telephoned Q.C.H. Put out feelers for a locum trainee. If the right man comes he can stay on.'

Philip had returned to Stockholm with the Petersens.

132

The builders were making good progress at the Manor and Blackie, after a month's rest and treatment, insisted that she would soon be fit for work again. So Nell had no pangs of conscience at leaving Lanmore and a fierce urge to do so before Philip came home again.

'Westhampton's less than an hour's drive from here,' she told her grandfather, 'and my off-duty's good. Alternate nights and alternate weekends, and one half day a week in addition.'

'They'll work you to the bone,' Andrew warned, from his own experience in obstetrics. 'Twenty-four hours on duty without a break, and you'll be lucky if you have four of them in bed.'

His forecast was proved only too right. Nell arrived at Westhampton on Monday morning at ten to nine, was swept up to the obstetric block by an enthusiastic young registrar, whirled round the department to meet the senior midwives and back to the main entrance to await the arrival of her chief, Mr Archibald MacFee, consultant in obstetrics and gynaecology. Mr MacFee was a genial and portly man, well into middle age. He extended a warm welcome to Nell as the newest member of his team, but after a couple of hours on his ward round she knew that genial he might be, tolerant of inefficiency never.

Until she got used to the routine it would be a tough job, and that was all to the good. She would have no time for brooding, no time for anything but total application to her work. Nell assisted at two Caesarean sections that night and tumbled into bed at four a.m., her unpacking still to be done. There was some respite in the morning, for the ante-natal clinic didn't start until ten, and blessed relief, her half day fell on Tuesdays.

'Which of course you won't need,' her registrar remarked at lunch, 'since you've only just started.'

Nell gave him an uncertain look, because she couldn't decide if he was joking. It was important not to start off on the wrong foot with her new colleagues.

There was laughter round the table, and Mr Watkins joined in. 'She thought I meant it! Of course you're free, Miss Ramsay. Make the most of it.'

Her grandfather was delighted to have her home again so soon and told her they would be able to return to the Manor in ten days' time.

'And Philip?' When does he come back?' She had had to return to his house when she gave up the job with the MacFarlanes.

The Colonel couldn't tell her, and Nell wondered if Philip's prolonged stay in Stockholm was due to Ilse Petersen. After thirty-six hours on her feet, however, she was too tired to pine. Once she was in bed she went out like a light, and only awoke when her alarm sounded at seven the following morning.

That first Monday at Westhampton set the pattern for all the days to follow. The obstetric residents were some of the busiest in the hospital. Their hours were gruelling but their work was rewarding, for midwifery wards were happy places. There were few mortalities in this day and age. The registrar told Nell they hadn't had a death in labour for five years.

'And that one should never have happened. A girl with a bad heart, who was warned she shouldn't have a child.'

Yes, labour wards were unlike anywhere else in a hospital. There was an atmosphere of joyful expectation, making the pain bearable and soon forgotten. Nell enjoyed her work and admired the midwives, those dedicated women who could be bossy on occasion, but who were worth their weight in gold. Especially the superintendent midwife, who terrified the younger nurses and not a few of the junior doctors.

'She seems to like *you*, Nell,' another houseman commented one day. 'Perhaps it's because you're such a serious girl, mind always on your work.' The way he said it made her sound dull and unattractive, thought Nell, but perhaps that was how he saw her, for she had plunged into her new work with a fierce determination to make a success of it, to drive Philip out of her mind by absolute commitment to her work.

On Thursday next she arrived back at his house to find him returned and having a drink in the sitting-room with her grandfather. His greeting was pleasant though without warmth. He gave her a critical stare as he handed her a glass of sherry.

'You look flaked out. Anything wrong?'

She was too tired to react to his unexpected presence. 'Why should there be? I was up all night, that's all.'

The men continued with their conversation. Nell took a sip or two of her drink and put it down on a small table. She rested her head on the back of the chair, closed her eyes for a moment and drifted off to sleep.

When she opened them again her grandfather had gone and Philip lounged opposite her, relaxed in his deep chair, one foot idly swinging. Some document lay open on his lap, but he wasn't reading it. He was studying her and smiling faintly.

She straightened abruptly, flushing under his gaze. 'Don't stare at me like that! I know I look a mess.' Her mirror had told her that this morning. There were deep shadows under her eyes and her hair needed washing.

'You never look a mess, Nell. You look a tired little girl, which isn't the same thing.' Unexpectedly he added, 'And you look very sweet when you're asleep. Ready to eat now?'

Nell glanced at the clock in dismay. 'You should have woken me. I must apologise to Mrs Reed.'

It was a more enjoyable meal than she had been prepared for. Elizabeth was out, rather surprisingly, since Philip had only just returned today and she had known when he was due back. Nell was still too weary to contribute much to the conversation, but it didn't matter because

Philip told them of his experiences in Sweden, which he knew well. The Petersens' name came up several times and over coffee he produced a packet of photographs—several views of Stockholm, a lakeside chalet, 'The Petersens!', a motorboat with someone at the wheel. 'Ilse! She sails well too.' A barbecue by a lake, and Ilse still glamorous, even in a large blue and white apron, waving a frying pan in the air.

'Does she cook well too?' asked Nell with an edge to her voice, and immediately regretted it.

'Superbly.' Philip's tone was bland and he gave her a smiling glance. 'Jealous, little Nell?'

'Of course not! What a stupid question.' Her voice was shrill and she knew that she had flushed.

'Oh, I don't know,' Philip said judicially. 'Most women find Ilse a little hard to take. So beautiful and so good at everything she does.'

The Colonel seemed to miss the undercurrents. 'Splendid young woman,' he agreed. 'Absolutely splendid, but perhaps a little lacking in ...' He sought for the right word ... 'Warmth,' he decided, and Philip's eyes went to Nell.

'Sex appeal, the old man really means,' he said under his breath, a remark which the Colonel missed, for he was becoming increasingly deaf.

This little interchange gave a much-needed boost to Nell's morale. Was it possible that Philip admired Ilse, but was not in love with her? That there was no physical attraction between them in spite of the girl's striking beauty? She longed with a painful intensity to be alone with him again, praying that her grandfather would go to bed before Elizabeth returned. All her good resolves were crumbling. She ached to feel Philip's arms around her. She no longer cared about what he thought of her, as long as he still desired her.

At nine o'clock the old man rose. Nell accompanied him upstairs, since Elizabeth was still out and he was not as steady on his feet as he had once been. When she returned to the sitting-room it was empty and Philip's study door was shut. Disappointment and depression swept over her and her eyes filled with tears. He had demonstrated very plainly that he didn't want her company. Common sense told her that he might well have work to catch up on, after his trip abroad. She blew her nose hard and tried to believe this, but there seemed no point in staying up, so she went to bed a few minutes later.

She had breakfast at seven-thirty and quite expected to be on her own, but Philip was down before her, eating bacon and eggs and reading a scientific journal, which was propped against the coffee pot. He put it aside when she came in.

'You look better for your early night. I was going to suggest a game of chess, but you were probably too sleepy to play.'

Nell's spirits rose at this information. With her eyes on her plate she observed demurely, 'Last time we played there was an unexpected ending!'

Philip leant across the table, put a thumb under her chin and tipped her face up. 'Unexpected, Nell? I should have said it was just what you expected.'

She flushed under his derisory glance, her happiness evaporating. How silly of her to make that remark, when she knew his opinion of her. She drained her coffee quickly and made to rise, but he put a hand on her arm.

'You've eaten nothing, you silly girl. You can't do a morning's work on an empty stomach.'

'I don't feel hungry.'

'Rubbish!' He poured her another cup of coffee, passed her the rolls, gave an unexpectedly charming smile. 'I didn't mean to offend you, but sometimes you're so touchy.'

Theirs would never be a smooth relationship, Nell thought, and gave a small unconscious sigh, head bent over her breakfast.

'What was that for?' Philip asked quietly. 'The sigh, my dear?'

She didn't look at him. 'I was thinking what a pity it is that we can't get on, since we have to see so much of each other.'

He had finished his meal. 'Cheer up,' he said briskly. 'You won't be here much longer,' and he walked out of the room.

'And thank goodness for that!' she said loudly, and was immediately ashamed of her rudeness, for Philip had been kindness itself to her grandfather and her aunt. The little incident niggled away while she finished her breakfast. She collected her things for the journey and on a sudden impulse, knocked on the door of Philip's study.

'Come in,' called an impatient voice. 'Mrs Reed, you'll have to start cleaning somewhere else.' He was at his desk, hunched over a file, pen in hand. While she hesitated, he crossed a line out, scribbled something in the margin and adjusted his spectacles. She started to back out and without looking up he asked, 'Has Miss Ramsay gone yet?'

'Going,' Nell said under her breath, and closed the door softly.

Seconds later it was flung open and Philip stood there, a frown on his face. 'I didn't realise it was you. What do you want?'

Spectacles altered his face completely, made him look older, more forbidding. A stranger. She wished he would take them off. She wondered how she could ever have made that flippant remark at breakfast to him. 'Well?' he snapped. Nell made a helpless gesture and he whipped his glasses off with a scowl. 'I'm hellishly busy. If you've something to say, say it.'

He kept a hand on the door, ready to shut himself into his study again. Woodenly she made her apology and he gave an irritated laugh. 'Was *that* all?' And what a waste of my valuable time, his tone implied. 'I'm so used to snide remarks from you I hardly notice them.'

The great day came at last when the family could return to Lanmore Manor—plastered and painted, the old oak floorboards newly stained and varnished, the kitchen hardly recognisable as the favourite room of her childhood. Nell had mixed feelings about it all.

'I liked it better as it was,' she sighed, when she returned on Friday night for her weekend off duty.

'That's because you didn't have to work in it,' Blackie said tartly, running a loving hand over the pale blue work surfaces, that had replaced the old scrubbed wooden tops.

'Elizabeth likes it?'

'Your aunt would like anything that raises its market value. She's been at the old man ever since we came back to get an estate agent out, find out what it's worth.'

'And Grandpa?'

'I thought he'd have a stroke when she suggested it. "Can't you wait till I'm gone?" he asked. He was in such a rage I thought he'd cancel the party.'

The party was to celebrate their return to the Manor and to show off its renewed glory to the neighbours. Standing in the drawing-room on Saturday evening, Elizabeth pointed out the beauty of the freshly painted ceiling moulding to her guests. 'Don't you think they've done it well? They've picked it out in gold and green to show it up more clearly.'

'Show up the dust as well,' muttered Blackie, who was circulating with a tray of savouries, and Elizabeth gave her a sour look.

'Blackie is definitely past it,' she announced, while the old woman was still in the room. 'We let her come back, but I doubt if she'll be up to it.'

'Aunt Elizabeth, hush!' Nell cast an anxious glance in Blackie's direction. Mrs Middleton-Massey was more forthright.

'You're a fool, Elizabeth, talking like that. You'll never get anyone else to run this great barn of a place.'

Elizabeth looked annoyed for a moment, then decided to agree. 'Exactly what I keep telling Father, but he's hopelessly pig-headed.'

It was a problem that Nell had met all too often as a doctor, old people clinging to unsuitable homes, knowing it would be sensible to move, but dreading the tearing up of roots that went deep into the past.

'Elizabeth, don't go on about it,' she said under her breath. 'It upsets Grandpa so. We'll manage somehow for as long as he's alive.'

'You mean I'll manage,' Elizabeth answered acidly, and Mrs Middleton-Massey clapped her on the shoulder.

'Don't make a martyr of yourself, my girl. Nell's home a great deal nowadays.'

'And spends most of it in bed!'

This was a marked exaggeration, though Nell had gone to bed at nine on Friday night, since she had had no sleep at all on the Thursday.

Determined to be agreeable, she said quietly that her obstetrics job would only last six months, and after that she would take something less demanding. She moved away to talk to the Middleton-Massey girls, who were chatting to Bobbie Fenton at the other end of the room. James and his young sister were staying with Philip again.

'Though much good it does me,' sighed Bobbie. 'They've spent most of the time working.'

Nell looked over to Philip, where he sat beside her grandfather near the fire.

'He's just about the most attractive man I've met,' enthused Bobbie. 'Don't you agree, Nell?'

Nell managed a creditable shrug. 'I suppose so, though I like your brother better,' and leaving Bobbie staring after her she walked over to James.

She was speaking the truth, for liking didn't come into

her feelings for Philip, indeed half the time she felt she almost hated him—for the powerful hold he had on her, and for his assumption that she reacted to other men's love-making as she did to his. She had never responded to any other man so passionately, and now she wondered if she ever would.

She talked to James and gazed at Philip, when she thought she could do so unobserved. He looked tired. Once he hid a yawn behind his hand. Once he glanced her way and she quickly turned to James.

'I'm sorry. Say that again,' she apologised, and James gave a wry smile.

'You've only been giving me half your attention for the last ten minutes. I wonder why?'

He was too nice for such offhand treatment. Nell coloured and stammered an apology, then she couldn't resist adding, 'Isn't Philip well? He looks rather pale.'

James' grave gaze held hers. 'So that's the distraction! I thought it might be. He's all right, just tired. We've been working very hard all week.'

'And all weekend, if Bobbie's to be believed.'

'Poor Bobbie,' he murmured. 'I'm afraid she's been very bored.'

'You should have sent her over here. I'd have welcomed her company.'

'Thanks, my dear girl, but I doubt if she'd have come. As long as there's a chance of seeing Philip she hangs around him. Wasting her time, of course, when he's involved with someone else.'

Nell put out a hand and gripped the back of a chair. James' face swam in front of her. He was saying something and looking very concerned.

'I'm all right,' she managed. 'I—I felt dizzy for a moment. Sorry.' Then with an effort, 'You—you mean Philip's engaged or something?'

'Or something,' he agreed with a faint smile. 'You know,

we shouldn't really be discussing him like this. He wouldn't like it.'

He accompanied this gentle rebuke with a worried look, that made Nell feel she had exposed more than she had intended to him.

Nell returned to Westhampton on Monday, tired and depressed.

'What do you do at weekends?' asked her registrar, Steve Watkins, over lunch. 'You look absolutely worn out.'

She missed sleep on duty because of her work. Off duty she stayed awake because of a man, a difficult unkind man, who was involved with another woman. Not engaged, if she'd understood James correctly. She longed to ask him what he had meant, who it was. Ilse or some other girl she knew nothing about? Philip travelled widely, met a great many people. He was, as Bobbie had said, a very attractive man. He had an aura of success about him, and that, coupled with his physical appeal, was a very potent combination.

There was laughter round the table. Nell jerked herself back to the present, and the realisation that the laughter was at her expense.

'She hasn't heard a word we've said,' remarked one of the women residents, and they all exchanged smiling looks.

One rather plain girl didn't smile but said caustically, 'Nell's too grand to muck in with us. Any time now she'll be sitting at the consultants' table.'

'Shut up, Judy,' Steve Watkins said. 'That was quite uncalled-for.'

'Was it?' Judy asked carelessly. 'Sorry, Nell, but you do rather keep to yourself. We never see you off duty.'

Nell had never had a reputation for being standoffish in the past and wasn't happy to have acquired one now. She tried to explain about her home commitments and they listened politely, but without much interest. Why should they be interested? she thought, relapsing into an unhappy silence. She was not the outgoing friendly girl of the Q.C.H. days. Unhappiness had made her withdrawn and aloof, quiet, dull probably, to this lively young bunch of doctors.

It wasn't a nice feeling being an outsider. She resolved to make more effort to mix with them, at least when she was on duty. On her next half day she thought she might as well stay in Westhampton, since her car was out of action and the train service was bad. On Monday night she telephoned home and spoke to her grandfather.

'I'll be home again on Thursday, Grandpa. You don't mind, do you?'

Her grandfather sounded disappointed. 'Elizabeth will be out. It would have been nice to see you.'

So Nell said she might come after all, but it would depend on the morning trains back. 'I have to be here by nine sharp. That's when my ward round starts.'

Half an hour later Philip telephoned. 'Your grandfather tells me you've no transport. As it happens I'll be in Westhampton tomorrow. You can come back with me.'

She agreed to meet him at three o'clock at the main hospital entrance. 'But are you sure you're not just coming on my account?'

'My dear Nell,' he said dryly, 'do you think I'd drive two hours there and back for the sake of your company? Would you for mine? No, of course I have business in Westhampton. See you tomorrow, then.'

After lunch next day Nell pottered about her room, washed a few underclothes, tidied her books and ended up in the common-room. She had half an hour to wait for Philip, so she might as well start to get on more friendly terms with the other residents. There were always a few young doctors around, either off duty or waiting to be called.

'Not going home today?' asked one of the house physicians.

'I'm waiting for a lift.' Nell was still chatting to him when there was a knock on the door and one of the porters looked in.

'Thought you must be here, Dr Ramsay. There's a visitor for you. I tried to get on to you, but the line was engaged.'

Her opposite number on the obstetric unit had been using the telephone for the last five minutes. Nell fished around for her shoes, which she had taken off when she curled up on the sofa. Philip must have come early. As she got to her feet he walked past the head porter.

'Hallo, Nell. I finished earlier than I expected.'

He stood in the doorway, smiling pleasantly, his glance flicking from her to the other residents, a big man, who created an impression as soon as he walked into a room. Nell could tell that her colleagues were burning with curiosity to know who he was.

'Mr Trent, a neighbour of mine,' she introduced him, picked up her overnight case and moved towards the door.

Philip seemed disposed to linger, looking around the shabby, untidy room with a smile, asking what the rest of their quarters were like.

'Just as bad,' said a cheeky young resident. 'If you're thinking of donating something to charity, remember us!'

Philip grinned. 'Who knows, when our factory in West-hampton is fully functioning, it might be good for our image! A new wing, with "Donated by Trent Electronics" on the foundation stone.'

It was a joke, but Nell knew that he was genuinely interested in medicine. As they drove away from the hospital she asked him when the factory had opened.

'Last week. Our policy is to expand in the Midlands, and even our main office will be moving from London to Birmingham next year.'

Nell digested this information with mixed feelings. It seemed that even at work she was to be reminded of his presence, for on their way out of town they skirted Westhampton's new industrial estate, and Philip pointed out the newly completed factory and the giant hoarding that said 'Built by Westhampton Construction Company for Trent Electronics.' She came this way herself. How could she have missed it?

Philip drove fast and didn't seem disposed to talk, though he was pleasant enough. Pleasant but remote. Nell thought what a fool she had been, getting worked up beforehand about this trip, but the thought of even an hour alone with him had been something that she couldn't view with indifference.

They were nearly home when he asked an unexpected and surprising question. 'Have you any idea what I've done to offend Elizabeth?' She stared at him and he went on impatiently, 'You must have noticed that she's been rather cool towards me lately. Any idea why?'

Nell thought she knew but didn't care to tell him. All those recent occasions that her aunt had been out when Philip was around—they were Elizabeth's way of showing that she didn't care—about Ilse or Bobbie or any other woman, with whom he might be involved. Infatuated she might be, but Elizabeth had pride. She was not her father's daughter for nothing. Only the brittleness of her manner these days was an indication of how much she was paying inwardly for this show of independence.

'Well, do you know?' Philip asked again, and Nell shook her head, for however she disliked her aunt she could scarcely humiliate her by disclosing her secret. 'Odd,' he mused, slanting a quick look at her. 'It reminds me of the way you used to avoid me.'

'Really?' He was getting dangerously close to answering his own question, and Nell sought for some other topic of conversation.

He brushed aside some trivial remark. 'Perhaps I offended her by standing up for you.'

She gazed at him with surprise. 'I'm astounded to hear that you ever did. When was that, Philip?'

He shrugged. 'Oh, some time when she was complaining about you taking this job at Westhampton. I only said that you deserved some life of your own. Probably that's what's wrong with her. She's touchy and intolerant because she leads such a narrow life.'

'I thought you liked Elizabeth.'

'I do, but I'm not blind to her faults,' he said evenly. 'I've known for a long time that she's partly responsible for the antagonism between the two of you. Six of one and half a dozen of the other, as they say.' He was silent for a minute or two and then came out with another remark. 'Pity she never married. Must have been a good-looking woman in her youth.'

'Thirty-eight is not exactly old,' Nell returned, filled with a deep pity for her aunt.

'As young as that?' He sounded surprised. 'I thought she was over forty.'

'Poor, poor Elizabeth!' thought Nell. Those casual remarks of Philip's swept away a pile of misconceptions. He had never been interested in her aunt as a woman. He looked on her only as a friend, and would have been astounded to learn that Elizabeth had once had other ideas.

CHAPTER TEN

NELL had to put up with a good deal of teasing when she return to Westhampton.

'Enjoy your night out?'

'Thought you said you were going home?'

'Some neighbour, you lucky girl!' That was one of the female house surgeons, who had witnessed Philip's arrival in the common-room.

In just such a way they teased the unmarried men doctors about the nurses, so Nell felt she was wasting her time trying to explain. 'He is my neighbour. He's a friend of my grandfather's.'

They jeered at that. 'And my aunt's,' she persisted. 'He is not my boy-friend.'

'O.K., we believe you, but don't give up hope.' Steve Watkins, her registrar, patted her kindly on the shoulder. 'We'd better go and have another look at that case of pro-tracted labour. Can't spend all day discussing your love life!'

'Well, honestly!' Nell exclaimed indignantly, as she raced after him down the long corridor to the obstetric block. 'It wasn't me who brought it up in the first place.'

He slowed down and gave her a friendly grin. 'I know, and they're a terrible bunch, but they don't mean any harm. Just curious about you, because you're such a mystery girl.'

'In what way?'

'In the way you behave. So aloof. So withdrawn. Judy thinks you're a snob.'

Judy was his girl-friend. 'I hope you don't agree with her.'

'Reserving judgment,' he said pleasantly. 'Now, about

that young woman . . .' and they turned from private affairs to the wider world of the patients.

James Fenton called on Nell one evening, when she was on duty at Westhampton. 'I was in the hospital, so I thought I'd look you up.'

'Visiting a patient?'

'Meeting an old friend—Alex Mackenzie. You know him, of course?'

Nell knew of him, but junior residents didn't have much to do with the consultants outside their own departments. When she said this James smiled and told her that Alex had married his house surgeon. 'A charming girl, and just right for him. He's much more human these days.' He went on to explain why he had called. Would she care to have dinner with him and the Mackenzies one evening? Make it a foursome? There was quite a decent hotel a mile or two outside town.

Nell accepted with pleasure and they fixed it for next Friday, which was the beginning of her weekend off duty. She enjoyed this rare evening out, for James was an excellent host, and she liked his friends once she had overcome a slight awkwardness at dining out with a consultant, who was so far above her in the medical hierarchy. She guessed that the other residents would make an issue of this, and said as much to Jean Mackenzie when the two girls were doing their faces after dinner.

Jean laughed. 'You don't have to tell *me*! I've been through it all myself. Half the hospital must have known about Alex and me, even before we announced it.'

Looking at her pretty, smiling face and hearing the tenderness in her voice when she mentioned her husband's name, Nell felt a bitter pang of envy. How wonderful to be happily married, to have found someone to care for and to have that caring returned. Had Philip spoilt her for other men? Was she never going to get over him?

On the drive back to the hospital she asked James the question that had been plaguing her for weeks. 'Is Ilse the girl that Philip cares about?' She blurted it out without any warning and could have bitten out her tongue a moment later. Into an embarrassing silence she stammered an explanation. 'I—I know it's none of my business. I only wondered. You did say he was involved with someone.'

James' lips were pursed, his expression very forbidding. 'That was most remiss of me. I'm surprised you remembered it.' And even more surprised that she had brought it up, his tone implied. He was being stuffy and rather prim. Or a loyal friend to Philip, depending how you looked at it.

'I'm sorry I asked,' muttered Nell, hot now with embarrassment.

When they reached the hospital car park she got out quickly. 'It was nice. Thank you.' That was all she could manage.

James walked round the car to stand beside her. He gave her a long thoughtful look, and his severe expression softened. 'I'm sorry, Nell, I should have been more understanding. For what it's worth I don't think it's Ilse. And that's all I can tell you until Philip chooses to say more.'

Until he announced his engagement, James meant, though perhaps Philip was a confirmed bachelor and chose affairs, rather than matrimony. Though if so, thought poor Nell, on the never-ending treadmill of alternating hope and despair, why then should he reject what she had to offer?

He had talked of an apartment he had recently taken in Westhampton for the use of himself or his associates. She wondered if he had used it yet. It caused her a pang to realise that he might be staying in the same town as her, and she knew nothing about it.

'Is Philip away?' Nell asked on her next Sunday at home, for they were to have lunch at the Manor.

Her aunt nodded, face a tight mask. 'As usual these days.'

They were in the kitchen together, Nell at the sink, arranging flowers. 'Can I ask Pamela round? She cheers things up.'

Elizabeth paused in the act of putting away dishes. 'Do we need cheering up?'

'Well, you seem a bit down ... and Pamela makes us laugh. Even Grandpa likes her, in spite of her weird clothes.'

'I'm not in the mood for that silly girl,' Elizabeth snapped.

Once Nell would have taken up the cudgels on behalf of her friend, tried to make Elizabeth alter her mind, started an argument that would have ended in a row. That their conversation developed into something worse than a row was due to quite other causes. She was worried about Elizabeth, whose manner was that of a person on the edge of a nervous breakdown. After a moment's hesitation she decided to risk a rebuff.

'Elizabeth, I've been worried about you lately. You don't look very fit.'

'I'm all right.' Elizabeth's face was averted and her hands twitched nervously.

'You don't look it,' said Nell gently. 'Wouldn't it be a good idea if you saw Dr Mac?'

'No!' Her aunt sank into a chair and now the twitch had spread to her face.

'Please, Elizabeth. If you don't see someone you'll make yourself really ill, and then how would we cope?'

'So that's why you're so concerned,' Elizabeth said bitterly. 'I might have guessed it.'

Wishing she had chosen her words more carefully, Nell said quietly, 'Well, it would upset Grandpa, but that's not the only reason. You are my aunt and I don't like to see you so ... off colour. Please see Dr Mac.'

'No!' Elizabeth banged her fist on the table in a quite uncharacteristic gesture. 'No, no, no! Sandy's the last per-

son I'd go to. He'd only say "I told you so."' She burst
into a storm of weeping. Her face streamed with tears, and
between great shuddering sobs she talked incoherently.
About Philip and how he had let her down, about the way
be flaunted his girl-friends before her, a dozen wild accusa-
tions uttered with increasing hysteria. Nell stood by the
sink, horrified by this outburst, while her aunt raved on
and on. When she stopped at last Nell crossed to her side
and laid a hand on her shoulder. 'I'm sorry Elizabeth. I'm
sorry.' Inadequate words, but spoken from the heart.

Elizabeth struck her hand away. '*You're* sorry! Do you
think I don't know that you're after him yourself? Much
good it'll do you, though. He's quite plainly not the marry-
ing kind,' and she started to sob again.

'Elizabeth, please. You'll make yourself ill. Go and lie
down—I'll get the lunch.'

When she visited her aunt's room two hours later Elizabeth lay on the bed, her face still ravaged by weeping, her
usually careful make-up grotesquely distorted. Frightened
by her appearance, Nell telephoned Dr MacFarlane and
when he came led him quickly upstairs. She knocked on
the bedroom door, opened it and gave a gasp. Elizabeth was
sitting on the edge of the bed now, shoulders hunched like
an old woman, and in her hand was a bottle of sleeping
pills.

Dr MacFarlane sat down beside her and took the bottle
from her hand. 'You've not taken any, my dear?'

An infinitesimal shake of the head, then Elizabeth's lips
started to tremble. 'Nell shouldn't have called you. I must
look . . . absolutely awful.'

Dr MacFarlane put an arm round the shaking shoulders
and drew her tenderly towards him. 'Not to me, Elizabeth.
You could never look awful to me.' Over Elizabeth's head
he saw Nell, transfixed in the doorway, and waved her away
testily.

Before Nell could shut the door on them she heard

Elizabeth give a great sob, saw her press her head against the doctor's shoulder. 'Oh, Sandy, I've been such a fool! Such a fool!'

Dr MacFarlane's words were cut off by the closing door. Astounded by the implications of this scene, Nell went slowly downstairs to reassure her grandfather that it was nothing serious. Her aunt had a bad migraine, and they would be having lunch on their own.

When Dr MacFarlane appeared at last Nell walked to the car with him. 'I feel absolutely terrible,' she said unhappily. 'It was all my fault going on about her looking so unwell. If I'd kept my mouth shut——'

'A good thing you didn't,' the doctor said briskly. He looked strained but happy. 'It was bottling it all up that was making her ill.'

'All that talk about Philip. Was there ever any truth in it?'

'Shouldn't think so for a moment, but women on the brink of middle age sometimes get strange ideas. Imagine themselves in love with younger men. She started an early menopause, you know.'

'Should I stay at home tomorrow?'

The doctor shook his head. 'Go back to work. Elizabeth will be all right now. I'm hoping to arrange a seaside holiday for her. My sister in Pembrokeshire has plenty of room, and if she can have us I'll run Elizabeth down, stay a few days myself. Andrew can manage with the new trainee.'

'Dr Mac ...' Nell hesitated over the words. 'Elizabeth and you ...' She found she couldn't go on.

The doctor clapped her briskly on the shoulder, face a shade redder than usual. 'None of your business, my girl.' He cleared his throat, opened the door of his car. 'Things have a way of sorting themselves out!' And on this platitude he departed.

He called again that evening to see how Elizabeth was

doing, and to tell her that he had fixed up the holiday with his sister. What her grandfather thought about it all Nell didn't know, though Blackie had plenty to say when she arrived back at ten o'clock, after her day out.

'Seen it coming for years. She's lived on her nerves far too long. Don't you worry, Nell, I'll look after the Colonel while you're away.'

So Nell left as usual the following morning, but felt obliged to see Elizabeth before she went. Her aunt was sitting up in bed, sipping tea, and looking at her calm composed face Nell found it difficult to believe that she had witnessed such disintegration yesterday. That the calmness was only skin deep she realised, when she saw the clenched hand lying on the silk coverlet.

'Well . . . I'm off,' she said awkwardly. 'Have a good time on holiday. You've earned a rest if anyone has.'

'Thank you, Nell. And . . . thank you for calling Sandy yesterday . . . even though I asked you not to.'

They exchanged a long look. Elizabeth seemed on the brink of saying something more, to be undergoing some inward struggle that cost her dear. Nell waited uncertainly, then Elizabeth sighed, gave her head a little shake and went on with her tea.

'Goodbye,' Nell said quietly. 'Dr Mac should be here in a couple of hours,' and she withdrew.

She had a hard day at work, but by seven-thirty there was a temporary lull on the obstetric unit. There were no deliveries impending and no new admissions to see.

'Corned beef hash,' grumbled Steve Watkins. 'I can't face it tonight. How about popping down the road to the White Lotus?'

The White Lotus was a Chinese restaurant of good repute. The residents used it frequently when they were on duty, for the proprietor willingly accepted hospital calls. A party of them went out, and a few minutes later they were

sitting in the bar, while they waited for their order, the
people on duty limiting themselves to beer or cider or soft
drinks.

Nell was sipping a tomato juice, perched on a high stool
between two young men doctors, when Philip walked into
the restaurant. He was alone, and casually dressed in slacks
and a thin sweater. He crossed to the counter and ordered
take-away food for one.

'Would you like a drink while you're waiting, sir?' the
dainty Chinese girl asked, and he nodded and came to the
bar.

When he saw Nell his eyebrows went up. 'Well, hallo!'
He looked at the two young doctors, taking in the arm one
of them had flung round Nell's shoulders in a half teasing
gesture. Nell wriggled uncomfortably, but the arm
tightened.

'Let the girl go,' reproved the other young man. 'You're
embarrassing her, you idiot.'

The house physician took his arm away with an exaggerated sigh. Philip watched this byplay with a sardonic
expression, and Nell wondered why he had had to come in
at just that moment. The house physician wasn't really interested in her. He had just been fooling, but Philip probably saw it as another example of her come-hither approach
to men.

'Off duty?' he asked down the length of the bar.

'No, we just couldn't face the awful hospital food. If I
was off duty I'd go home.'

'Come and join me,' he suggested, so Nell carried her
tomato juice along and took the vacant stool beside him.
'Don't you think you're overdoing it, going home every
time you're free? Got a guilt complex about all those years
you neglected them?'

'No, I haven't,' snapped Nell. 'But with Elizabeth away
I have to go home. I can't leave it all to Blackie.'

'I didn't know she was having a holiday.'

'Not a holiday. She's unwell.' She would have been content to leave it at that, but he wanted to know more details. He probed and Nell parried his questions.

'Is there some mystery?' he asked impatiently. 'Why do you have to be so secretive about it?' He sat easily, one elbow on the bar, successful, good-looking, healthy in mind and body. Nell remembered her aunt's ravaged face. The trauma in her mind she could only guess at, but she felt a sudden urge to punish Philip for what he had done.

Completely forgetting Dr MacFarlane's view of the situation, she blurted out angrily, 'If she's ill it's all your fault. You **must** have known what you were doing to her.'

He gave her an astonished look. 'Are you mad or am I? What am I supposed to have done to Elizabeth?'

Nell glared into his handsome face, quite oblivious of the interested stares of the others, though she did have enough discretion to lower her voice. 'Made her fall in love with you, of course, as if you didn't know.'

His reaction was unexpected. Astonishment gave way to mirth. He was still laughing when the Chinese girl handed him a paper carrier. 'What a funny girl you are, Nell. Elizabeth and I . . . the idea's ridiculous!'

'Is it?' Nell asked stormily. 'Perhaps it is to you, but it isn't to her. Wasn't anyhow. She seems to have realised what a fool she's been,' and she turned her back on him and walked away.

Their meal was ready now, so she joined the others at their table. When she looked towards the bar Philip had gone. As her anger evaporated, apprehension took its place, for she was beginning to appreciate the consequences of her indiscretion. She had lost her temper and behaved unforgivably—given away Elizabeth's secret, though mercifully Philip didn't seem to believe her. Could she retrieve the situation by an apology? Say that perhaps she had imagined it? She was still trying to make up her mind when she got back to the hospital, but Philip forestalled her by telephoning first.

'Nell? I want to see you. Tonight!' He was curt to the point of rudeness.

She stammered out the information that she was on duty, and couldn't leave the building.

'Really?' he said with sarcasm. 'Then what were you doing at the White Lotus?'

She explained about the arrangement with the proprietor, tried to placate him by apologising, suggested that she might have made a mistake. Her voice must have lacked conviction, for he paid no attention.

'If you can't come out I'm coming round. Expect me in fifteen minutes.'

'But, Philip . . . my night round!'

'To hell with your night round!' he snapped, and slammed the receiver down.

Nell's reaction was one of pure panic. She did have a night round, though she usually started it an hour later at ten-thirty. She left a message with switchboard that she was expecting a visitor, but had to go to the wards. 'Give him my apologies and tell him I'll get in touch tomorrow. Tell him I'll be quite a time, so it's not worth him waiting.'

The night staff were put out by her early appearance and didn't bother to conceal it. Only consultants were allowed to make their own rules. Ruffled by her reception, Nell shut herself into the ward office and read through a pile of case notes, with which she was already familiar. One of the staff nurses relented enough to make her a hot drink, and by eleven she felt it was safe to return to the residents' quarters. Exhausted by a long day, she looked forward to relaxing on her bed, though it was far too early to undress, since she was bound to be called out again.

She opened her bedroom door, found the light on and Philip sprawled in her one easy chair. He was reading, incongruously, a textbook of midwifery. 'How . . . did you get in?' she asked nervously, as he rose to face her.

'The porter has a master key.'

'I didn't think you'd wait. You did get my message?'

'Yes, I got it,' he said grimly. 'And now if you can spare me a few minutes——' He took her by the shoulders and thrust her into the chair, standing over her in a distinctly menacing way.

'Philip, please sit down,' Nell said faintly. 'You make me nervous looming over me like that.'

'I hope I am making you nervous,' he said savagely. 'I could hit you, my girl, for the trouble you've caused. How many people have heard that ridiculous story from you?'

'None,' she whispered. Unnerved by his anger, she forgot the white lie she had intended telling. 'It isn't a ridiculous story,' she excused herself. 'Older women often f-fall in love with a younger man.'

He brushed her remark aside contemptuously. 'You have a distorted sense of humour, my dear Nell. I suppose Elizabeth told you how she feels! I can just imagine that!'

'Yes, she did,' Nell answered quietly, 'and she was very unhappy about it. In fact she was on the brink of a complete breakdown, which is why Sandy's taken her off to Pembroke.'

She watched his scepticism disappear, to be replaced by uneasiness. He walked to the window and back, frowned down at her. 'Dr MacFarlane believes this—this extraordinary story?'

'Yes, he does,' Nell said steadily. 'Because it's true.'

She could see that she had convinced him. He stared at her, silent for a minute or two, and when he spoke his voice was bitterly contemptuous. 'So it's true, and how you must have enjoyed it! You realise it'll be impossible for Elizabeth and me to meet now without embarrassment?'

Horrified, Nell protested that she hadn't intended making trouble. 'I'm sorry, Philip. I should never had told you——'

'Then why did you?' he ground out, and she made a helpless gesture. She couldn't explain that momentary impulse. Even to herself it was difficult now. 'But I didn't mean to make trouble,' she offered miserably, and he gave an angry and disbelieving laugh.

'Didn't you, Nell? I think you saw a perfect way of getting your own back on your aunt and me. You've never liked her, have you, in spite of all she's done for you? You've enjoyed humiliating her and embarrassing me.'

She started to rise, but he gave a hard shove so that she fell back into the chair. 'Presumably Elizabeth doesn't know that you planned to tell me?' Wordlessly she shook her head. 'Then keep it that way,' he said grimly, 'because if you don't, Nell Ramsay, you'll have me to reckon with.' He picked up the book on midwifery, dropped it back on to the table with a thud. 'I wish I understood what goes on in that mind of yours. You have an important and responsible job, which I suppose you do adequately or they wouldn't employ you. I'd begun to think that I might have misjudged you... that we might even become ... friends, but I like my girls honest ... and decent ... and you're neither. In fact you're a thoroughly malicious, twisted little bitch, and I'm sorry for any man who gets himself involved with you.'

He delivered this long speech with fierce intensity, gave her a searing look of dislike and contempt and strode out of the room. Nell was too drained emotionally to move from her chair, and when Night Sister rang to talk about a new admission she was still sitting in the same place, staring into the fire.

CHAPTER ELEVEN

IT was ten days before Nell saw Philip again. That he was avoiding her was very obvious, for whenever she was on duty he found time, however busy he was, to visit her grandfather. When she was home he stayed away.

'He's more and more at Westhampton,' the Colonel told her. 'They plan to move the main office from London even sooner than they originally intended. I think Philip always had it in mind when he decided to make his home here.'

Nell felt tired and dispirited, though she did her best to conceal it from the old man. She was sure that she had finally and irrevocably turned Philip against her, and she knew that this time it was entirely her own fault. What madness had got into her, to make her blurt out her aunt's secret? The truth was, she thought sadly, that when Philip was near her she was ruled by her emotions, and not by her intellect. The time had come when she must get a grip on herself, if she wasn't to degenerate into one of those self-centred, self-pitying females whom she had always despised.

At the weekend she took one of the Middleton-Masseys' horses out and rode all day through the Welsh border hills, coming to terms with her problems, facing up to reality. She loved a man who didn't even like her and she would have no peace of mind, let alone happiness, until she got over him. Hard work, plenty of leisure activities and a return to her normal social life were the antidotes. Full of good resolutions, which she hoped she would have the strength of mind to carry out, she returned home in the evening, to find Dr MacFarlane just arrived. He had come back from Pembrokeshire that morning, bringing news that astonished the Colonel, though Nell was half prepared for it.

159

Elizabeth and he had decided to get married next month. A quiet wedding, just family and close friends. When her grandfather had collected his wits he showed sincere pleasure, shook his old friend's hand, harrumphed and announced that Elizabeth was a lucky girl. He'd quite given up hope of seeing her off his hands.

'Mind you don't say that to Elizabeth,' Sandy rebuked. 'It's I who am the lucky one. I've waited years for this.' When he left he asked Nell to walk out to the car with him. 'I have a letter for you from Elizabeth. You can read it after I'm gone.' He fished in the glove compartment, handed her a pale blue envelope. 'Don't think too badly of her. Only a desperately unhappy woman would have done what she did.'

After he had gone Nell went into the stables, not wanting to read the letter in front of her grandfather, sensing that this was something private between Elizabeth and herself. Her aunt came straight to the point, no words wasted.

Dear Nell,

This evening I had a long talk with Sandy and he says that what I told him I must also tell you. That I won't feel at peace with the world until I do.

Did you never wonder why Father dealt so harshly with you? Why he wasn't prepared to make things up after the quarrel? He never had your letters, because I tore them up. He never knew about your phone calls, because I was always the one who answered. I told you he didn't want to speak to you, but he never had the chance. I knew he was too proud and stubborn to make the first move, but he was longing for you to do so.

I tried to tell myself that my motives were good, that I only wanted to protect him from further distressing scenes. I lied to myself, of course. I was jealous of you, Nell, just as I used to be jealous of your mother. I always felt that Father loved her, and then you, better than me.

I know that's no excuse, that you may well find it unforgivable. If so I shall understand, but I should like you to answer this. Sandy will have told you our news. He has loved me for years. I've known it for a long time, and I nearly lost him through my stupidity. What I thought I felt for Philip was madness, and I see now I had no right to blame him. I know I can trust you never to talk about it to anyone.

Please write soon,

Elizabeth.

P.S. I leave it to you whether you choose to tell Father.

Nell sat on an old pile of sacks with this extraordinary letter in her hand, and thought out its implications. She should have guessed long ago, not been content with letters and telephone calls. Elizabeth had always collected the mail while the Colonel was still in bed, and the old man scarcely ever answered the telephone unless told it was for him. She should have come down to visit them, had it out with her grandfather. If she had done so their estrangement would have been over years ago.

Some of the blame must be hers, though Elizabeth's behaviour had been unforgivable. Dr Mac had said 'Only a desperately unhappy woman would have done it', and once her first indignation was past Nell began to agree with him. She had studied psychology. She knew the unhappy results of sibling rivalry. She had learnt from her medical work how embittered a woman could become when she saw her chances of matrimony receding. Sandy was a dear, but he was stout, red-faced and balding. Beside Philip's virile good looks he must have seemed to Elizabeth a poor second best.

When Nell went into the house she knew what she must do. She shut herself into her bedroom, plugged in the telephone and put through a call to Pembrokeshire. When Elizabeth came on the line she sounded stiff with tension.

'You've . . . read my letter?'

'Yes.' Nell swallowed nervously and began. She told her aunt that she did understand, that it had all happened a long time ago, and that the best thing they could both do was to forget all about it, make a fresh start, try to be friends.

Elizabeth's voice was gruffer than usual. 'You're very generous, Nell. Especially as I—I haven't been very nice to you since you came back home again.'

An understatement, Nell thought wryly, but she didn't want to rake up the past. She suspected that much of Philip's dislike of her had had its roots in Elizabeth's mischief-making. That if her aunt hadn't been constantly on hand, making sly digs and deprecating remarks, they might have become friends long ago.

And then Elizabeth asked the question she had been dreading. 'You haven't told anyone, have you? How I felt about Philip?'

An old chief of Nell's had remarked after a ward round, on which a patient had asked if he had cancer, 'If you decide to lie, lie through your teeth, girl. No half measures about it or it doesn't ring true.'

Nell knew that if she salved her own conscience by being honest, she could wreck Elizabeth's hard-won peace of mind, make her aunt's future meetings with Philip horribly embarrassing, perhaps spoil the close friendship between Philip and her grandfather. So she obeyed her old chief's dictum and said steadily that of course she hadn't, and never would. Elizabeth could rest easy on that score.

'And ... Father? Have you told him anything?'

This was Nell's chance to make amends. In the stables she had been tempted. Now she knew that she couldn't betray her aunt a second time. 'What point, Elizabeth? It might make bad blood between you and Grandpa. I'd rather forget the whole business. Like I said, start again.'

She knew a momentary pang, quickly suppressed, when she thought how different things might have been if Elizabeth hadn't acted so maliciously. She would have made it up with her grandfather years ago, met Philip when he first came to Lanmore. He would have had no preconceived ideas about her. They might have been good friends. The attraction would still have been there, and if he had liked her it wasn't impossible to imagine him returning her love.

She pulled herself up sternly. Daydreams were for schoolgirls, and weakening to the character. The ifs of life were better not pursued. However, there was one thing she had to do before Elizabeth came back—let Philip know of the white lie she had told her aunt. That way they would both be spared awkwardness. Elizabeth had believed her, and Philip had enough sophistication to hide any embarrassment he might feel.

She couldn't face meeting him. Even a telephone conversation would be unnerving. In the end she settled for a letter, thinking as she wrote it what a lot of emotion her family was putting on to paper these days! She told him most of her conversation with Elizabeth, leaving out all the reference to her quarrel with her grandfather. She said she didn't expect to be believed, but she sincerely regretted her indiscretion. That she hoped he wasn't staying away from the Manor on her account, and ended that there was absolutely no need to reply. She just wanted to relieve his mind of any disquiet over Elizabeth.

In spite of her disclaimer she half hoped to hear from him, but he neither wrote or telephoned, and continued to stay away when she was at home.

July came in with a spell of hot humid weather, so that the delivery rooms at the hospital were like a furnace, and the medical staff longed for fewer babies to be born.

'Wouldn't you think they'd plan it better?' one of the midwives complained to Nell, as she bathed the latest arrival. 'Who wants a baby in a heatwave?'

Nell laughed, removed her cap and gown, and kicked off her rubber boots. She ran a hand through her curls because she had left her comb behind, and retired thankfully to the residents' quarters. She felt hot and sticky, badly in

need of a shower. As she turned the corner that led to the
staff block she gave a little gasp and came to a halt. Philip
was coming out of the residents' wing. She went slowly
towards him, the blood thundering in her ears.

'Were you looking for me? I've been on duty. Did you
get my letter? You did understand what I was trying to
say?'

He nodded, his expression cool. 'Yes, Nell, I understood.'

She sighed. 'I can see you haven't really forgiven me,
but all the same thank you for coming.'

'My dear girl, I hate to disillusion you, but I'm not here
on your account. Alex Mackenzie and I are working something out for the trauma unit. Trent Electronics are keen
to link up with medical research, and this is one of the most
go-ahead hospitals in the country.' He nodded casually,
and since she could only stand and stare stupidly up at him,
he put both hands on her shoulders and moved her out of
the way.

It was a cruel and deliberate snub, and she had laid herself wide open to it, by her idiotic assumption that he had
come to see her. All her good resolves, her determination
to be sensible, had disappeared as soon as she saw him.
At that moment she came near to hating him. Hurt and
humiliated, she climbed the stairs wearily to her bedroom,
hoping that it would be a long time before she met Philip
again. A vain hope, for he seemed to haunt the hospital.
She saw him in the distance next afternoon, talking to
Alex Mackenzie, passed his car in the drive another day,
went into the dining-room one Monday to find him at lunch
with the consultants.

Her cheeks burnt when she saw him there and she chose
a chair with her back to him, thankful that junior and senior
staff sat at separate tables. She scarcely noticed what she
ate, so conscious was she of the man behind her. The impulse to turn and look at him was almost uncontrollable.
She pushed away a half-eaten portion of marmalade tart

and rose clumsily. At the door she ment Jean Mackenzie, who greeted her with a friendly smile.

'Is the hospital food still as awful as it used to be?'

'I don't know,' Nell said foolishly, and Jean stared at her.

'Well, honestly! Are you so wrapped up in your work you don't even notice?'

'I—I mean I don't know what it used to be like, but it is pretty dire.'

Jean laughed. 'How I feel for you! Alex, we must ask this girl round to our place one evening. Give her some decent food for a change. Hallo, Philip! Nice to see you.'

Nell stiffened, and wished she hadn't stopped to talk to Jean. She kept her eyes on the other girl's face and hoped Philip would have the tact to walk on. He stayed where he was, almost touching her, making it difficult for her to behave normally. Alex was agreeing with Jean, saying she must certainly come round. Would Friday do? Fine. And then as an afterthought he added casually that Philip would be there too. 'You know each other, of course?'

It was too late to turn down their well-intentioned invitation, unless she could find some last-minute excuse. Resolved to do just that, Nell managed a stiff smile, caught the gleam in Philip's eyes and hurried away.

On Friday morning she woke with a vague feeling of disquiet, then remembered that it was this evening she was supposed to be dining with the Mackenzies. Could she change her duty hours? Find someone who wouldn't mind swapping? Pretend that it was a large last-minute emergency? But when she approached them none of the other residents wanted that evening off.

A headache? A heavy head cold? Too feeble. Her car had broken down? What was to stop her taking a taxi? In the end she was forced to admit that she had no valid excuse for backing out. She was off duty this weekend and planned to drive home after dinner, so at least she could leave early.

She dressed carefully, putting on a pretty ruffled blouse and a long cotton skirt besprigged with flowers, spent longer than usual on her face and armed with the knowledge that she looked her best, drove to the Mackenzies' house, which was in an outer suburb of Westhampton. By bad luck she arrived just as Philip was locking his car. Hoping he would go on ahead, she fiddled with various objects in her handbag, pretending to look for something, but when she raised her head he was still there, standing beside his car and watching her.

Reluctantly she climbed out and said an awkward 'Good evening.' Then she rushed on, 'I imagine you're no better pleased about this than I am?'

'About what?' he asked levelly, and she made an irritated gesture.

'Why pretend? I can't think you've been looking forward to my company.'

His smile was unkind. 'Since you want the truth you shall have it. If I could have thought of a good excuse I wouldn't have come. Unfortunately I couldn't.' His mouth tightened. 'They're nice people and they'd be horrified if they knew how we really felt. So they mustn't find out, must they?'

He thrust a hand through her arm and led her towards the house. It would have been an enjoyable evening if the man had been anyone but Philip. There were just the four of them, and after a delicious meal they sat out on the patio in the warm summer dusk. Nell hid her true feelings behind a gay and brittle mask, though she did her best to avoid looking at Philip, directing her remarks at Alex or at Jean. At ten o'clock she felt that she could decently make her farewells, since she had an hour's journey ahead of her.

'And I'm rather tired because I was up most of last night.'

Jean took her upstairs, and as they passed a half open door, asked if she would care to see the family. Looking at her pretty, smiling face, at the love and pride that shone out of it as she bent over the sleeping infants, Nell felt a lump in her throat. They were so close, the Mackenzies, so happy.

'How I envy you,' she whispered, and turned away quickly, to hide the tears in her eyes.

Jean straightened from tucking the blankets round her youngest son. 'What is it between you and Philip?' she asked quietly, and when Nell didn't answer, 'Forgive me for. being tactless, but I've a feeling we blundered, asking you together. Am I right?'

She was such a nice girl and there seemed no point in denying it. 'I suppose so,' sighed Nell. 'We ... don't like each other, though I didn't realise it was so obvious. I thought we hid it very well, considering how strongly we feel.'

'Oh, you did,' Jean assured her.

'Then how did you know?'

'When a man and a girl do their best to avoid looking at each other, when they're both young and attractive and unattached, there has to be a reason for it.' She linked arms with Nell and led her towards the top of the stairs. 'Pity, because I'd have expected you to have a good deal in common. Anyway, I'm sorry for giving you an awkward evening. Perhaps you'll come again when we have other visitors. I love to hear all the hospital gossip!'

They all came out to the drive to see Nell off, though Philip showed no sign of leaving yet. Thankfully she climbed into her car and switched on the ignition. Nothing happened. She tried again and then again.

'Don't keep doing that,' Philip called. 'Let me have a look at the engine.'

Five minutes later both men confessed themselves stumped, and Jean said, 'You won't get a garage to do anything at this hour. Drive her back to the hospital, Alex, and it can be looked at in the morning.'

Philip slammed the bonnet down. 'No need for you to bother, Alex. I was going home anyhow. She can come with me.'

Nell's protests that she would rather wait for her car to be repaired were swept away, and ten minutes later they were driving west towards the Shropshire hills.

She said unhappily, 'I'm sorry about this. I've broken up your evening, haven't I?'

'That's all right. I see a good deal of Jean and Alex.'

'Jean guessed about us.'

His hands tightened on the wheel. 'Guessed what, for God's sake?'

'How we feel about each other, of course.'

'Then she's a very clever girl,' he said dryly, 'because I'm not even sure how I feel myself.'

Nell turned to stare at him. What was he trying to say? When she stayed silent he went on slowly, 'You looked very sweet tonight, Nell. Very pretty and desirable. It's a pity your character doesn't match your appearance.'

She slid lower in her seat and looked out at the darkening countryside. 'You made up your mind about me even before we met,' she said tiredly, 'so nothing I say now will make any difference.' Just for a moment she nearly mentioned her aunt's letter, but she had done enough harm already, blurting out uncomfortable truths. 'I don't feel like talking. I really am tired.'

After that they drove in silence, and Nell was only half awake when they reached the Manor. Philip laid a hand on her shoulder and she sat up with a jerk. His face was within inches of hers. She gave him a sleepy little smile, stifling a yawn with one hand, her defences down, because she was so tired, longing only to be close to him. She touched his cheek lightly. 'Philip . . .'

He drew in his breath sharply. 'You look worn out. You'd better go to bed.'

He was round to her side of the car while she was still

fumbling with the door. A firm hand under her elbow
assisted her up, turned her towards the front door—getting
rid of her as quickly as possible, before he succumbed to
the attraction that flared between them whenever they were
alone.

'I'll take you back to Westhampton on Monday morning,'
he said briskly. 'Will eight o'clock be all right?'

She nodded, managed a subdued 'Thank you,' and
opened the front door. He was gone before she had crossed
the hall, and that was how it was going to be from now on.
He would spend no longer in her company than was absolutely necessary. Any overtures on her part would be firmly
repulsed and if she wanted to avoid further humiliation she
must never, never forget it.

She had told herself this a hundred times already, but
the truth was that reason urged her one way, her emotions
another. Her good resolves were forgotten when she was in
Philip's company.

The weekend dragged by. On Sunday afternoon the door-
bell rang and Nell jumped to her feet, heart beating faster.
She opened the door with trembling fingers, to find Mrs
Middleton-Massey standing there.

'Hallo, Nell. Hope this is a convenient time to call? I
haven't seen your grandfather for quite a time.'

Stifling disappointment, and despising herself for feeling it, Nell led her into the sitting-room, where she and her
grandfather had been reading the Sunday papers. Inevitably
the conversation turned to the news about Elizabeth.

'Sandy told us. Brave man, taking on that daughter of
yours,' Mrs Middleton-Massey snorted, with supreme lack
of tact.

Her grandfather scowled, and Nell cut in quickly, 'That's
so unkind! I'm sure they'll be very happy.'

'Are you, miss?' rejoined the older woman sharply.
'Since when have you been on Elizabeth's side?'

Nell flushed, hesitated, and said lamely that there were always differences of opinions in families, but that she and her aunt understood each other better these days.

Their visitor's expression was sceptical. The Colonel thumped his stick on the ground. 'Damn it, Roberta, d'you have to be so tactless? Known you forty years and you've no more wits than you had as a young girl!'

Not a scrap offended, his old friend roared with laughter. 'Never pretended to be brainy, Edward. Left school at sixteen, thank God! Got married at eighteen! This is the first time I've had you two alone together since Nell came back, and there's something I'm longing to ask.' She leant forward in her chair, a stocky woman with sturdy legs planted a little apart.

Nell thought wildly, 'What is she going to say *now*?'

'I've always wondered why you took so long to make things up. Your grandfather's a pig-headed old man, Nell, but I thought you were more sensible. I'd have expected you to make the first move.'

'But I did——' Nell blurted out, taken off guard by these unexpected remarks, then she broke off in mid-sentence, swallowed, stammered and started again. 'That is, I did mean to, but—but I thought—I thought—oh, for heaven's sake! Do we have to rake up the past like this?'

'I wish you had written,' her grandfather said gruffly.

'Perhaps she did,' Mrs Middleton-Massey remarked, gazing at the ceiling. 'Letters can get . . . lost.'

'Not in this country,' the Colonel countered sharply, staring hard at his granddaughter. 'You didn't write, did you, Nell?'

Nell had never been a convincing liar. Crimson with embarrassment, she poked at the small log fire that the old man liked even in summertime. When the front door bell rang a second time, she jumped up thankfully. This time it *was* Philip, casually dressed in sports shirt and jeans, another visitor enquiring about her grandfather.

'I haven't seen the old man for several days. How is he, Nell?' He looked at her flushed cheeks and raised his brows. 'Something wrong? Have I picked a bad time to call?'

'Oh no, no! Come in, Philip!' At least if he was here Mrs Middleton-Massey would surely be more discreet. He looked surprised at this reception, but made no comment as he followed her into the sitting-room. 'I'll get tea,' said Nell, and made for the kitchen.

She took her time about it and when she finally returned with the trolley, she got the impression that they had been talking about her. They all looked towards the door, and there was a little silence, broken by Mrs Middleton-Massey.

'See what I mean? If my girls looked like that I'd do something about it.'

'How do you like your tea, Mrs Middleton-Massey?' asked Nell, hoping to divert her from further personal remarks.

'Milk first. No sugar. I was just telling these men that you're looking peaky. And far too thin.'

'I work quite hard,' Nell said mildly, and started to pass the teacups around.

'So you need a rest when you come home,' finished Mrs Middleton-Massey, who wasn't easy to deflect. 'And you don't get it with your grandfather to look after.'

'I like looking after Grandpa.'

'And that huge garden an endless struggle! Never looks tidy however much you do.'

'I know, but I do my best. And I enjoy gardening. It's good relaxation after my medical work.' She was very conscious of Philip's scrutiny, intent and unsmiling. Perhaps he thought she had been grumbling to Mrs Middleton-Massey before he came. When tea was over she excused herself, saying that she wanted to spray the roses. She was filling a container from the tap in the stables when she heard voices from the front of the house.

Looking through the archway, she saw Mrs Middleton-

Massey and Philip standing together, talking earnestly. They drew apart as she approached and said their goodbyes.

'See you at eight tomorrow, Nell.' Philip raised a hand in casual farewell, and moments later his car followed the other one down the drive.

Nell was uneasy all evening in case her grandfather referred to that afternoon's conversation. She kept out of his way as much as possible and chattered when she couldn't avoid him. When she looked into his bedroom last thing at night, she gave him a quick peck on the cheek, but before she could retreat he caught her by the hand, his bony old fingers surprisingly strong.

'You're a good girl, Nell, keeping your mouth shut like that. Roberta means well, but she's damned indiscreet. Want to talk about it, now that we're alone?' The faded blue eyes were intent under bushy white eyebrows.

'No, Grandpa,' Nell said gently, 'I don't.'

There was relief on the old man's face. He patted her hand fondly before he let it go. 'Wise girl. There's been a lot of water under the bridge since then. Does no good to rake up the past.'

As she prepared for bed Nell felt happier than she had been for weeks. Her grandfather and she understood each other now, for all that so many things had been left unsaid. The last shadows cast by that old quarrel had been swept away for ever.

On the drive to Westhampton next morning Philip said very little. He looked abstracted, remote, frowning now and then as if he was wrestling with some problem. Nell knew that the link-up with the hospital had involved him in a heavy extra work load, and she wondered, not for the first time, how he managed to look so fit on it.

She thanked him as he drew into the hospital car park, apologised for taking him out of his way and opened the car door.

'Nell.' He caught her by the arm, holding her back. 'Are you working too hard? Was the old girl right?'

'Mrs Middleton-Massey talks too much,' Nell said lightly, and gave a tug of her arm. 'I don't work any harder than you do, I'm sure.'

His fingers tightened. He frowned down at her. 'That's different. I'm a man.'

'Oh, really, Philip! What an outdated viewpoint!'

'Yes, I suppose it is,' he admitted, rather to her surprise. 'But you're such a little thing.' Again that intent frowning look. 'I wonder if I've misjudged you, Nell—about a whole lot of things.'

As always when she was close to him, Nell's heart started to hammer and her thoughts became scattered. 'I have to go,' she said under her breath. 'I start work at nine.'

'Oh, damn your work!' Philip exclaimed irritably, but he took his hand away. He was out of the car as quickly as she was, staring at her across the width of the bonnet.

'Roberta told me things I find hard to believe, though they would make sense of a good deal that's puzzled me.' He hesitated for a few minutes. 'I had a picture of you in my mind before we met. I though you'd be tough and ambitious and not at all feminine—all the things I dislike most in a woman.'

'And you haven't changed your mind,' Nell said sharply 'You called me some very rude names that night in my room.'

He sighed. 'I know, and I'm sorry, but I was shaken by what you told me about Elizabeth. Why did you tell me Nell? Why? Why?'

'You know why. Because I'm malicious and ungrateful Because I've always hated Elizabeth.' Nell spoke wildly be cause she didn't like the direction in which their conversa tion was heading. If Philip persisted with these awkward questions she was in danger of blurting out the truth.

'Roberta thinks you have good reason to dislike you

aunt,' he went on quietly. 'Is that true?'

'I would rather not talk about it, Philip.'

He banged his fist on the bonnet of the car in frustration. 'But I want to talk about it. When are you free next?'

'Not till tomorrow.'

'What time? I'll pick you up.'

She stared in surprise. 'What's got into you, Philip? What have we got to talk about?'

'You know what,' he answered very quietly. 'We can't go on like this, if I'm to retain my sanity!' Perhaps he felt his words were too melodramatic, for he flushed slightly. 'How I wish we'd met under different circumstances,' he added slowly.

'It would have made no difference,' Nell said bitterly. 'You were determined to dislike me from the word go.'

His smile was crooked. 'Self-protection, my dear girl. And you know why I needed it.'

He didn't have to spell out the strength of the attraction between them. It was there most potently on that bright summer morning, so that Nell longed to be alone with him and despised herself for her longing. He had made her so unhappy, hurt and humiliated her so often. If she accepted the olive branch he seemed to be offering it could only lead to further unhappiness. She would be back on the same seesaw of emotions, vulnerable and confused.

A car swept by and drew into the bay marked with Mr MacFee's name. 'My boss!' Nell exclaimed with relief. 'I must dash.'

His fingers closed around her waist. 'Not until you agree to meet me.'

Mr MacFee was climbing out of his car, glancing in their direction, Nell tugged, but Philip held on. 'I can come round tonight,' he said. 'You name a time.'

'Oh, for goodness' sake, Philip!' she snapped in a furious undertone. 'Let me go. He's wondering what's going on.'

'What time?' he persisted.

'No time. It's not convenient. I'm bound to be busy and even if I wasn't——' She broke off and he waited for her to continue, still holding her wrist, while Mr MacFee finished locking his car and started walking towards them. 'Even if I wasn't I wouldn't want you round. You have a bad effect on me—as if you didn't know.'

Her cheeks were flushed now and she threw a quick glance at Mr MacFee, who was passing by not ten feet away. 'Good morning, Miss Ramsay,' he said benignly. 'We start in two minutes. Hallo, Trent. You seem to haunt this place!'

'I know, sir, and I'm just coming,' Nell called as he walked on, and to Philip indignantly, 'So let me go ... and ... and stop looking like that! It isn't funny.'

His smile made him appear years younger. 'You're working yourself up into a great rage, dear girl. You want me to come round all right, but you're afraid to admit it.'

'Of course I'm not. I really am busy when I'm on call.'

'Then come to my apartment tomorrow evening,' he said and her breath quickened at the expression on his face. If she went to his apartment he'd make love to her, for she wasn't strong enough to resist him. She was tempted but determined not to give way.

'Oh, Philip,' she sighed, 'if only I could make you understand! You want an affair, but I—I want——' Her voice faltered. She took a long deep breath and started again. 'If you love a man you want something more permanent. Something more than just a physical relationship.'

She broke off, appalled by her own words, at what she had just given away. 'So now you know,' she said hoarsely, gave a choked little sob, and ran towards the hospital entrance, leaving Philip staring after her.

CHAPTER TWELVE

THAT evening Philip telephoned to ask once again if he could come round. Nell was snatching a brief respite from the labour wards, relaxing on her bed, pillows piled behind her head.

'What for?' she asked warily.

'Just to talk.'

'I can't think what we have to talk about.'

'Look here, Nell——'

'I'm sorry, Philip, but I'm first on call and frightfully busy, so if you don't mind I'll say goodbye.' She put the telephone down, and disturbed by Philip's call, crossed to the window. It was open and she sat on the sill, staring down at the people who were streaming out of the main entrance at the end of visiting time. Once she would have welcomed any contact with Philip, agreed eagerly to his suggestion, but after her confession in the car park, she felt she would never be able to face him again. She was surprised that he had bothered to telephone, but decided with unusual cynicism that her admission, far from embarrassing him, had acted as an encouragement. If she loved him, he must be reasoning, then she would not hold out long against his advances.

He had never made any secret of the attraction he felt for her. He had said he regretted the way they had first met. If only they could put the clock back, Nell thought sadly, how different things might have been. She dragged her thoughts back to reality, and reminded herself that from now on she was going to concentrate on her work. She would avoid emotional entanglements, play it cool, try to enjoy life once again, as she had done in her student days.

When Philip telephoned again at midday on Tuesday, she agreed that it was her half day, but she had to dash home. Pamela Middleton-Massey was coming round. 'Pity,' said Philip, sounding very frustrated. 'I can't leave Westhampton, but I thought we might see each other for an hour or two before you went home.'

'Sorry, I'm afraid I can't.'

On Wednesday she met him at teatime in the doctors' dining-room, accompanied by James Fenton. She greeted James with more warmth than she showed to Philip, asking what brought him there. She hadn't realised that he was concerned with the technical side of electronics.

'Someone has to work out the cost of all the complicated gadgetry this chap designs,' James said dryly, jerking a thumb in Philip's direction.

'Join us, Miss Ramsay,' Alex Mackenzie suggested, and after a moment's hesitation she did so, taking the chair beyond James, which was well away from Philip.

'I've talked your boss into utilising some of Trent's ideas,' remarked Alex, and Nell stared at him in surprise.

'Mr MacFee? He hasn't mentioned it to us.'

'He will,' Philip said firmly. 'So you'll be seeing me on the obstetric unit soon.' The glance that accompanied these words was challenging.

The others lingered over their tea, but Nell had a young woman in labour, on whom she wanted to check. 'Excuse me,' she murmured to James, but as she left the table Philip followed her into the corridor.

'When are you going to let me talk to you, Nell?'

'We're talking now.'

His mouth thinned and he looked as if he could have shaken her. 'You can't avoid me for ever, my girl. Don't you want to hear what I have to say?'

She shook her head, 'Not particularly. I gather that I'm no longer your pet hate, but it's a little late for friendship, and I don't want what you have to offer.'

Before he could reply she turned and walked quickly away, and that was the last she saw of him for a couple of days, though Mr MacFee talked about Trent Electronics on his next ward round.

'Have to move with the times, I suppose.' He didn't sound especially enthusiastic. 'Their designer wants to look around the block, get some idea of our special requirements.'

On Friday afternoon, when Nell was checking a new admission, a young nurse brought her a message. 'You're wanted in Mr MacFee's office when you're free, doctor.'

'Would you tell Mr MacFee that I'll be down as soon as I've finished with this patient.'

'It's switch on the line, doctor, but I'll ask them to pass it on.'

The new admission was very young, very nervous and desperate to see her husband. 'They're calling him from work, doctor. He promised he'd stay with me right through.'

She was a healthy girl, so the examination was quite straightforward, but because she was so apprehensive it took Nell longer than usual. Half an hour had elapsed before she made her way to the ground floor and knocked on Mr MacFee's door. There was such a noise in the corridor that she barely caught a 'Come in.' She walked into the room and stopped dead when she saw who was there.

Philip! He was leaning back in her chief's swivel chair, hands locked behind his head, a triumphant smile on his face, and he was the only person there.

'Shut the door, Nell,' he said pleasantly.

She left it open. 'Is this your idea of a joke?'

'My dear girl, hasn't your boss explained to you that I'm going to be around the obstetric unit for the next few days?'

'Yes, he has, but I can't see how I can help. The Registrar would be more use.'

'Not for what I have in mind,' Philip said softly, and stopped the chair in midswing and was around the desk while she was still trying to decide what to do. He pushed the door shut with his foot, caught her by the hands and jerked her into his arms. Outraged, Nell shoved at his chest.

'Let me go! Anyone could come in—Mr MacFee! This is his office.'

'He's loaning it to me for a few days,' Philip smiled, controlling her struggles easily, 'But if you're afraid of interruptions I'll lock the door,' and he did just that.

Nell tore herself away from him and backed round the desk, aware of the fact that the obstetric wards overlooked this office, acting on the assumption that he would hardly try to make love to her in front of possible witnesses. 'If you touch me again, Philip, I'll—I'll——' She could think of no threat to deter him, and scowled when he laughed.

'All right, Nell, perhaps I should have talked first and acted afterwards, but I've been pretty riled by your behaviour.'

'*You've* been riled by *my* behaviour! Please unlock that door. If someone came along it would look very odd, us being locked in here.'

He grinned but unlocked it, though he kept his back against it. 'What I have to say won't take long. You can't be that busy or you wouldn't have come down.'

She sighed and sat herself on the edge of the desk. She had to hear him out some time. Perhaps it would be as well to get it over. 'All right, Philip, I'm listening.'

For such a positive person he seemed to be having some difficulty in starting. 'You're angry with me, Nell, and I suppose you have good reason. I've ... not been very kind to you, have I? Jumped to conclusions too quickly. Not listened to your side of things.'

She kept her head bent, staring at the intricate pattern of the carpet.

'So I'm sorry. Deeply and sincerely sorry. And I hope very much that we can start again. You talked about friendship the other day, but you must know, my dear girl, that it's not friendship I want. You said you loved me too.'

A tremor passed through Nell, but she still wouldn't look at him. He left the door and came to stand before her. If she had put out her hand she could have touched him. She locked them together to resist the impulse.

'I know exactly what you want, Philip, and once I'd have given it to you. Once I'd have been delighted to hear what you've just said. But I'm tired of being torn to bits emotionally. I don't want an affair with you, or with anyone else for that matter.'

'Nell, darling.' She weakened at the gentleness in his voice when he said that.

'I have to go,' she whispered, and rose unsteadily, straight into his arms. His kiss was gentle too and against her will her arms crept round his neck. One hand stroked his thick dark hair.

'Oh, Philip,' she sighed, and his hold on her tightened, his mouth became more demanding.

Afterwards she decided that the knock on the door was a good thing. Philip swore softly and let her go. It was James, and Nell was very conscious of her flushed cheeks and untidy hair. She interpreted James' amused look correctly. He knew quite well what they had been doing.

'I—I must dash,' she stammered.

Philip said quickly, 'No, Nell, not yet——' but she was already half through the door and running down the corridor.

If he had said he loved her in return, would she have weakened? He had a powerful hold over her physically. Would she have run away from his apartment if they'd been alone, just the two of them, with no chance of interruption? She knew that she would not have done, that her strength of will would not have been equal to it. That she would have gone to bed with him willingly, though she would have regretted it afterwards. She didn't want to become just another girl-friend, the girl of the moment because she was available. Because they were both working in Westhampton and Ilse was in Stockholm.

Next weekend Nell was on duty. On Saturday morning she was having coffee when Alex Mackenzie walked in. There were only a few people around and when he saw her he came to sit beside her.

'Nice place, your home,' he said casually, and Nell stared at him.

'You mean the village? Have you been through it recently?'

'I mean your home. Trent took me there yesterday afternoon.'

'Really?' Before she could ask any more questions a house surgeon told her she was wanted on the telephone. An urgent call to the labour ward, and by the time she came back Alex had gone.

Probably Philip had taken him to his own place to discuss work, and they had called on her grandfather on the way. The weekend was an especially busy one, and when she came off duty on the Monday she had forgotten all about it.

Although she was no longer on for emergencies she had her routine ward work to do, and an ante-natal clinic in the afternoon. This was not too demanding, which was just as well since she felt very sleepy—blood pressures to check, various tests to be done, queries to be answered. An ordinary afternoon's work in a busy clinic.

At five o'clock Nell swallowed a cup of tea in Sister's office and decided to have a couple of hours in bed, since she had been up most of last night. She hung her white coat behind the door, slid out of her dress, drew the curtains and crawled thankfully under the bedclothes, clad only in her slip. Her room was hot, because it faced west and got the evening sun. Too hot to sleep, she thought, tossing back the blankets, then she thumped her pillow into a more comfortable shape and shut her eyes.

The telephone bell brought her back to consciousness, and her grandfather came on the line before she was properly awake. His voice was gruff, his manner brusque.

'That you, Nell? Have to tell someone the news. Elizabeth and Sandy got married this morning in Pembrokeshire. Decided they wanted a quiet wedding. Might have let their families know, dammit!'

The old man sounded very upset, so Nell spent several minutes soothing him down and trying to make him understand the couple's actions. 'You know what Dr Mac's like, Grandpa. He hates any fuss. He must have talked Elizabeth into it.'

'Then she must really love him,' grunted the Colonel. 'I'd have expected her to want a big wedding with all the trimmings.'

'Which would have cost a fortune,' Nell pointed out. 'So you should be glad they did it this way.'

'I suppose so,' he conceded reluctantly. 'Though it would have been something to look back on when we've left Lanmore.'

'Left ... Grandpa, what are you talking about?'

'Hasn't Philip told you yet? He said he'd be seeing you when he got back.' The old man was silent for a few moments, then he told her sadly that he had come to the conclusion they could no longer live at the Manor. 'I've known it in my heart for a long time, dear. And now, with Elizabeth gone and you away working, it's ridiculous for me to stay here. Blackie can't go on much longer and where would I find someone to replace her?'

'Oh, Grandpa, stop it, stop it!' cried Nell, close to tears. 'It would break your heart to sell Lanmore. You mustn't even think of it.'

'To sell it, yes,' the Colonel agreed, 'but renting it wouldn't be so bad. Particularly in such a good cause.' He went on to explain that Alex Mackenzie had been searching for just such a house to turn into a convalescent home for his orthopaedic patients. It was Philip who had suggested Lanmore. They had visited the Colonel last Friday, put the idea to him, and he had spent the weekend brooding over it.

'My mind's made up, Nell,' he said briskly. 'I've already discussed the legal side of it with my solicitor, and he's contacting the Area Health Authority for me.'

'But nothing's signed?' queried Nell. 'Please wait till I've been home. Please don't do anything rash, or you're sure to regret it.'

'Not a complete fool,' growled the old man. 'Been thinking about moving for a long time, Nell. I'm grateful to Philip for coming up with such a good idea.

'Philip!' thought Nell furiously, when the old man had rung off. It would be Philip, poking his nose into other people's affairs. Influencing her grandfather to make a decision that he would most likely regret, when it was too late. She had a vivid mental picture of orthopaedic convalescents at the Manor, old people in wheelchairs, physiotherapists in the library, Alex's crippled children in the garden. The Colonel would hate it, though she knew there was a great need for more convalescent homes. But somewhere else, for goodness' sake! Some other house. Not the beloved home of her childhood.

She worked herself up into such a state that there seemed only one thing to do—go and see Philip, tell him what she thought of him and his bright ideas. She understood now why he had wanted to talk to her. The lovemaking had probably just been a softening up process, she thought bitterly, too upset to think rationally.

She drove round to his place. She knew the address, for he had told her previously. A modern block of apartments, five minutes from the hospital. Only when she had pressed his bell did she wonder if it wouldn't have been better to telephone first.

It was eight o'clock; he might have visitors. In sudden panic Nell hoped that he was out. She stared uncertainly at the gleaming white door with the neat name-plate, in two minds whether to go or to stay. She had left it too late, however, for the door swung open and Philip stood there.

He looked surprised to see her, then as he took in her stormy expression, a rueful smile appeared. 'Hallo, Nell, this is an unexpected pleasure. I think I can guess why you've come.'

'Clever you!' snapped Nell, and swept past him with head high.

An open door showed where the living-room was, and she was relieved to see that it was empty. 'Just as well you haven't got visitors. We can quarrel in private.'

She stood in the middle of the room, scowling at him. 'You've got a nerve, Philip Trent, interfering in our affairs! Grandpa would never have thought of leaving Lanmore if you hadn't put this—this ridiculous idea into his head.'

'You do him an injustice,' Philip said calmly, shutting the door and turning to face her. 'He's discussed it with me more than once in the past, even before you came back. He felt he was being selfish to Elizabeth, clinging on to a past way of life, when she would have preferred a more modern house.'

'Elizabeth's out of it now. She and Dr Mac got married today.'

He raised his eyebrows. 'Good for them! But there's still your life to consider. Can you honestly say you've enjoyed trying to cope with that old-fashioned house and that enormous garden?'

'It's better since we had it renovated.'

'Better, but too big for such a small family. Besides, when you marry——'

'I'm not thinking of getting married.'

He walked towards her and she backed away nervously. His eyes were very bright and a smile hovered on his lips. He knew how attractive he was, Nell thought crossly, and took a deep steadying breath.

'Keep away from me, Philip! If you touch me I'll—I'll scream!' At his incredulous look she flushed. 'Well, I'll stamp on your toes or—or do something.' Her flush deepened when he started to laugh.

'Darling Nell, what a fool you are! You know perfectly well you like it when I kiss you. And so do I,' he added softly, reaching out a hand towards her.

'Leave me alone!' Nell exclaimed. 'If you have any decency you'll do your best to undo the damage you've done. Tell Grandpa the house isn't suitable after all.'

'But it is, perfectly suitable. You should be pleased to think it can be put to such good use instead of lying empty and decaying.'

'It won't decay if we're in it.'

To her relief he dropped on to the sofa. 'You can't put the clock back, Nell. Your grandfather has made up his mind. It was a hard decision, but he's made it, and he won't retract. Besides, when you get married——'

'I've already told you——'

'So you have, my darling girl.' He rested his head against the back of the sofa and gave her an unexpectedly sweet smile. 'I've been a complete fool, Nell. A jealous, unreasonable fool, thinking you were involved with Andrew Mac-Farlane or that lad from Q.C.H. Of course you're going to get married, and soon, dear love, before you drive me completely round the bend.' The smile became both tender and ironic.

Nell stared at him in astonishment, wondering if she could possibly have misunderstood him. Could he mean—did he mean—'Oh, Philip,' she gulped, 'don't play games. I can't bear it!'

He held out both hands to her. 'Come and sit down, my love. I was never more serious in my life. I've been trying to ask you to marry me for days.'

She collapsed on to the sofa, shaking and incoherent.

'Stop babbling,' Philip said gently, and took her in his arms. When she was calmer and able to accept the incredible, the joyful fact that he loved her and wanted to marry her, Nell rested her head against his shoulder with a sigh.

'I suppose you're right, darling. Grandpa couldn't stay there on his own, but where will he go?'

'He'll live with us, of course. I have plenty of room.'

'I don't think he'd like that.'

'Once he's got used to the idea he'll agree. In fact at the risk of sounding conceited I think he'll be pleased.' His mouth quirked. 'If I hadn't thought so I wouldn't have taken Alex out to see him.'

She jerked upright. 'And what if I hadn't agreed to marry you? Where would he have gone then?'

'But you have agreed, sweetheart,' he said blandly, and she felt a small spurt of annoyance. 'You not only sound conceited, you are conceited, Philip Trent! It would have served you right if I'd turned you down.'

'But I knew you wouldn't, my love, after what you told me in the car park.' He pushed her back against the cushions and said thickly, 'How soon will you marry me, Nell? Don't keep me waiting much longer.'

Overwhelmed by physical sensation, she shivered with pleasure at his touch. 'We don't have to wait, Philip,' and then, as his face tautened, 'I'm off duty tonight, if you want me to stay.' Blushing and suddenly shy, she turned away from him. 'Don't look at me like that! I've never said that to any other man. In fact, though you probably won't believe me, I've—I've never had an affair with any man.'

'I do believe you,' Philip said quietly. 'It was only when I didn't know you very well that I listened to Elizabeth's malicious gossip. That woman has a lot to answer for, but I suppose I have to wish them happiness. Sandy's a decent man at any rate.' He put an arm around her and drew her against his shoulder. 'No, little one, we'll wait until we're married. I couldn't face your grandfather if I had a guilty conscience!' Smiling, he looked down at her. 'Though I've been tempted more than once, I don't mind admitting.' He ruffled her hair lovingly.

Nell caught sight of herself in a mirror. 'Good heavens, what a mess I look!' Hair tousled, cheeks flushed, she turned to him worriedly. 'Oh, Philip, I'm not at all the sort of girl you ought to marry.'

'Really? What sort of girl would suit me?'

'Oh, you know! Someone smooth and sophisticated, mad about clothes. The sort of wife that's an asset to a business man.'

'But I'm not a business man,' he said gently. 'I'm an engineer. However, we'll try to find a suitable wife for James.' He was laughing at her, and after a few moments she joined in.

'Ilse might do,' she suggested, sobering suddenly, and waiting anxiously for his reaction.

He shrugged. 'James finds her as lacking in appeal as I do.'

'She's very beautiful,' Nell insisted, unable to leave the subject alone.

'What are you trying to ask? Was I ever in love with her? No, nor ever more than superficially attracted. Her father was a business associate, that's all.'

'Pamela Middleton-Massey told me once that you have hordes of girl-friends.'

'I've collected quite a few in my travels,' he admitted. 'What is this, Nell? An inquest on my past life?' His voice was cool now.

'Please, Philip, don't be angry with me. I've been jealous too, thinking of you swanning round half the capitals of

Europe with gorgeous girls like Ilse.'

His expression changed, became amused and tender. 'My darling girl, what a vivid imagination you have! I've been far too busy to spend much time with women. And when I did it meant nothing. Just an evening's relaxation.' The doorbell rang and he rose. 'That'll be James—I was expecting him. Just as well perhaps, or I might have accepted your offer!' As he crossed to the door his smile grew broader. 'You're the only girl I know who still blushes!'

The moment he was gone Nell jumped to her feet, tore open her handbag, ran a comb through her hair and straightened her clothes. She heard the two men talking in the hall, and as the door swung open, moved quickly away from the mirror.

James' usually serious face was transformed by his rare smile. 'Philip has just been telling me the news, and I'm very glad to hear it, Nell.' He looked from one to the other of them. 'Strange,' he said reflectively, 'how even the most intelligent people can behave like complete idiots when they fall in love!'

Philip punched his old friend in the chest. 'After that remark you don't deserve it, but stay and have a drink with us, then we must telephone the Colonel. Champagne! There's some left from the party we threw for those Dutch engineers.' He disappeared into the kitchen, whistling cheerfully.

Nell looked after him lovingly, then caught James' eye. 'I hope it won't give Grandpa too much of a shock! He's had one today already.'

'My dear girl,' said James dryly, 'he would have to be blind, and much deafer than he is, not to know there was something between you two. Perhaps now Philip will be able to concentrate on his work again. He's a very brilliant man, Nell, and sometimes he can be difficult, but you're absolutely right for him. I have no doubt about that.'

Nell flushed with pleasure. 'Thank you, James. That's

the nicest thing anyone has ever said to me,' and then Philip came back from the kitchen, the champagne bottle under one arm.

The cork popped and the champagne fizzed out. James raised his glass to them both, Nell standing secure in the circle of Philip's arm.

'All the best for the future. I know that you'll be happy.'

Harlequin Romances

The books that let you escape
into the wonderful world of romance!
Trips to exotic places...interesting
plots...meeting memorable people...
the excitement of love....These are
integral parts of Harlequin Romances—
the heartwarming novels read by
women everywhere.

Many early issues are now available.
Choose from this great selection!

Choose from this list of Harlequin Romance editions.

449 **Come Back, My Dream**
Elizabeth Hoy

454 **Such Frail Armor**
Jane Arbor

464 **The Captain's Table**
Alex Stuart

469 **Maggy**
Sara Seale

494 **Love Is My Reason**
Mary Burchell

500 **Unsteady Flame**
Marjorie Moore

513 **Far Sanctuary**
Jane Arbor

516 **Prisoner of Love**
Jean S. MacLeod

528 **Wife by Arrangement**
Mary Burchell

532 **To Win a Paradise**
Elizabeth Hoy

538 **Strange Request**
Marjorie Bassett

557 **The Time Is Short**
Nerina Hilliard

597 **This Much to Give**
Jean S. MacLeod

604 **Flight to the Stars**
Pamela Kent

627 **With All My Worldly Goods**
Mary Burchell

643 **A Life to Share**
Hilary Preston

658 **Reluctant Relation**
Mary Burchell

711 **My Heart's in the Highlands**
Jean S. MacLeod

712 **House of Conflict**
Mary Burchell

730 **The Stars of San Cecilio**
Susan Barrie

766 **The Enchanting Island**
Kathryn Blair

796 **Hibiscus House**
Faye Chandos

800 **Sweet Waters**
Rosalind Brett

802 **South to Forget**
Essie Summers

804 **Bladon's Rock**
Pamela Kent

805 **Love This Enemy**
Kathryn Blair

856 **Too Young to Marry**
Rosalind Brett

861 **Bewildered Heart**
Averil Ives

890 **Two Sisters**
Valerie K. Nelson

892 **The House of the Swallows**
Juliet Armstrong

895 **And Falsely Pledge My Love**
Mary Burchell

901 **Hope for Tomorrow**
Anne Weale

904 **Moon at the Full**
Susan Barrie

911 **The Return of Simon**
Celine Conway

918 **These Delights**
Sara Seale

MEDICAL ROMANCES

409 **Hospital Corridors**
Mary Burchell

430 **Ship's Nurse**
Alex Stuart

438 **Master of Surgery**
Alex Stuart

443 **That Wonderful Feeling**
Elizabeth Gilzean

446 **Borne on the Wind**
Marjorie Moore

451 **Air Ambulance**
Jean S. MacLeod

462 **Love from a Surgeon**
Elizabeth Gilzean

468 **Star Quality**
Mary Burchell

478 **Dear Trustee**
Mary Burchell

485 **Island Hospital**
Elizabeth Houghton

489 **Flower of the Nettle**
Jane Arbor

491 **Sally in the Sunshine**
Elizabeth Hoy

495 **Nurse with a Dream**
Norrey Ford